"Do you, Samantha Telford, take Perseus Kostopoulos to be your wedded husband?"

"Yes." *With all my heart*, she murmured inwardly. No matter how bogus this wedding might be, she loved Perseus. Her part of the ceremony would not be a lie.

The pressure of his hand seemed to tighten a fraction before the priest asked in a solemn voice, "Do you, Perseus Kostopoulos, take Samantha Telford to be your wedded wife?"

"I do," came the fervent response. Perseus was such a wonderful actor; he sounded as if the vows actually meant something to him. In the next instant he removed the flower garland from her lace-covered head. A strange smile hovered at the corners of his compelling mouth as he found her left hand and placed a ring with one exquisite teardrop-shaped diamond on her finger.

"Make no mistake, *Kyria*. We're married in the eyes of God and the world. I'm your husband now."

Everybody loves a wedding: they're romantic and exciting.
And in our WHIRLWIND WEDDINGS miniseries we have
weddings that are more exciting than most!

WHIRLWIND WEDDINGS is a series that combines the
heady romance of a whirlwind courtship with the joy of a
wedding—strong heroes, feisty heroines and marriages
made not so much in heaven as in a hurry!

Titles in this series are:

REBECCA WINTERS: Rebecca, an American writer and
mother of four, is a graduate of the University of Utah. She
has also studied at schools in Switzerland and France,
including the Sorbonne. Rebecca is currently teaching
French and Spanish to junior high school students. Despite
her busy schedule, Rebecca always finds time to write.
She's already researching the background for her next
Harlequin® romance!

Rebecca Winters

Bride By Day

Whirlwind Weddings

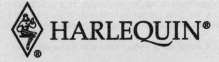

HARLEQUIN®

TORONTO • NEW YORK • LONDON
AMSTERDAM • PARIS • SYDNEY • HAMBURG
STOCKHOLM • ATHENS • TOKYO • MILAN • MADRID
PRAGUE • WARSAW • BUDAPEST • AUCKLAND

ISBN 0-373-03519-5

BRIDE BY DAY

First North American Publication 1998.

CHAPTER ONE

"I'M SAM Telford from Manhatten Office Cleaners. My employer told me you wanted to see me."

Samantha, who preferred to be called by the shortenend version of her name, had been forced to run all the way from her apartment, and had been caught in the middle of an early May cloudburst. She was dripping wet and didn't dare sit down on any of the upholstered chairs.

The elegant, middle-aged secretary looked at her with vague disdain. "Are you the person who cleaned this office last night?"

"Yes."

"Then you're the one. It's after two o'clock. You were expected in long before now."

"I was in class all morning. My boss didn't reach me until I returned to my apartment a little while ago. Obviously something is wrong."

"You could say that," came the cryptic reply. "Please, just…stand there for a minute."

Sam bit her bottom lip. She couldn't afford to be in trouble, let alone lose her only source of income. Right now she was literally down to her last hundred dollars, and was counting on her next paycheck. At this point she was grateful for her job, and would die before she went begging to her father, a portrait painter of international repute who had never acknowledged her existence as a human being, let alone his daughter.

Through the art department she'd heard rumors that he was living somewhere in Sicily with his latest mistress.

Her jaw hardened. Someday, when she'd made a big success of her own artistic career—*and she would if it killed her*—she'd present herself to him. That day couldn't come soon enough for her. She was living for the moment of confrontation, not only because of its shock value alone, but because she couldn't wait to show him she'd made a success of her life, *without him.*

He'd gotten away with murder for years. *But not forever*, she vowed vehemently.

"Ms. Telford? Mr. Kostopoulos will see you now."

The head man himself?

Sam's nervousness increased. Kostopoulos Shipping and Export owned the impressive sixty-eight-floor office building located on the Upper West Side in New York City.

Trepidation set in as she walked through the double doors of the office she'd cleaned less than eighteen hours earlier. To her embarrassment, her tennis shoes squished on the marble floor, announcing her entry in no uncertain terms.

Automatically her eyes flicked to the wall. To her relief the Picasso was still there among a grouping of original oils and graphics. For a moment Sam had feared there might have been a theft during the night. It belonged in a museum like the D'Orsay in Paris where the whole world could admire it. Instead, it was part of a private collection only a privileged few would ever be allowed to see.

The simplistic yet charming painting of a pair of hands holding a bouquet of flowers had to be an original, though Sam recognized that it was an unknown version of Picasso's masterpiece, *Petit Fleurs.*

She imagined he'd paid a fortune to obtain such a treasure. Most likely there'd been private negotiations between the Marina Picasso family and Mr. Kostopoulos.

In the broad light of day, the room's clean yet exquisite Hellenic accoutrements deserved a second glance. But her curious gaze fell on the powerfully built male dominating the room. He was structured along the lines of a classic Greek god, and she couldn't look anywhere else. He was definitely *numero uno*.

His taut stance and tightened facial muscles led her to believe some very fierce thoughts were running through his mind. She shivered at the possibility those thoughts had anything to do with her.

He stood at the window, totally oblivious to the luxury surrounding him. His right profile was in evidence while he stared at some invisible spot only he could see.

Living in an artist's world of color as she did, Sam was immediately intrigued by his overly-long black hair. It put her in mind of an inky void no ray of sunlight dared penetrate. She imagined this was the color of darkness before God made the light.

Aquiline features and brows like eagle's wings made him an arresting figure. But to Sam's mind, it was the savage two-inch scar along his right jawline which quickened her interest. It appeared to be an old wound which had healed a long time ago, but stood out because he was a man who probably had to shave twice a day.

He didn't look like a person who feared anything. Quite the opposite in fact. Since he made more money than even most wealthy people probably found decent, why hadn't the scar been removed through plastic surgery?

Though perfectly groomed and wearing an expensive, hand-tailored gray silk suit, there was a primitive quality about him that hinted at untamed fires burning beneath.

She could well imagine anyone meeting him for the first time would speculate on the scenario which would have marred such an unforgettable male face—the kind of face she would love to sculpt if sculpting were her best medium.

"Come all the way in, Ms. Telford."

Suddenly Sam became the focus of his unsettling scrutiny. In one sweeping glance his inky black eyes took inventory of her form and feminine attributes, then he scowled. Apparently he found her attire as distasteful as her person.

Her five feet four inches felt very tiny and pathetic standing there in her sopping wet outfit which consisted of nothing more than scruffy jeans and an old denim shirt she hadn't bothered to tuck in. Decorated with a print from her own handmade blocks, the pattern looked more like black cat's paws than odd-size circles, but Sam hadn't been displeased with the result.

Maybe it was her hair the imperious-looking man didn't seem to like. That morning she'd been in such a hurry to get her final art project to the university on time, she hadn't been able to find her favorite scarf.

For want of anything else, she'd been reduced to improvise, and had come up with a remnant from one of her originally designed, fishnet chains normally meant to hold hanging flowerpots. She had used it to tie back her thick, yellow-gold hair at the nape. If left unconfined, it flounced like an oversize mop.

"I'm in," she couldn't resist commenting because he was obviously trying to intimidate her.

The air crackled with tension. "My secretary said you were the person who cleaned this office last night."

He spoke impeccable English in the deepest voice she'd ever heard. Yet in spite of his less than friendly demeanor, she caught traces of his attractive Greek accent. *Let's face it, Sam. He's the most gorgeous male you've ever seen in your life, let alone your dreams.*

"That's right."

"What happened to the man who usually cleans this suite?"

"Jack went home ill, and asked if I would finish up."

He continued to stand motionless, feet apart. With her fanciful imagination, he could be the god Zeus, astride Olympus, issuing his latest decree. Sam thought he was closer to forty than thirty, yet she considered him young to run such a vast empire. If rumor among the night crew could be believed, legions of world-famous singers, models and movie stars had tried to become the wife of the mysterious Greek tycoon, but all had failed.

Of course it didn't mean that there wasn't a special woman somewhere in the cosmos who had a softening effect on him. Since Sam heard that he flew to Greece on a regular basis, she assumed he had a love interest in a beautiful woman from his own country and race. Someone who kept a low profile away from the public eye, and the *paparazzi*.

The woman would have to be incredibly brave to take him on... *And very lucky*, a tiny voice whispered.

"I'll get straight to the point. Last night, while in mid-flight between Athens and New York, a vitally important telephone call came in to this office. My secretary attempted to route it through to me, but there was too much static on the line, so she left the phone number on my desk. I drove here straight from the airport, only to discover that the note was gone."

He hadn't accused Sam yet, but the inference couldn't have been more clear.

She smoothed a damp tendril away from her forehead, all the while conscious of his inquisitive eyes following the movement of her hand whose broken nails and calloused, oil-stained fingers were a far cry from those of his immaculate secretary.

Sam had never been the kind of person to envy another woman. But for once in her life, she wished she had the kind of remarkable looks and polish to attract a man like him.

"I've been cleaning the offices in this building for the last six months, and know better than to touch anything. All I did was dust, vacuum, and scour the bathrooms."

His brows became a black bar of intimidation. "You saw nothing on this desk?"

Her eyes darted to the mirrorlike finish. Only a telephone was on display. For a man of Mr. Kostopoulos's legendary business acumen, she wondered how he ran his megacorporation with everything out of sight.

"No. It looked exactly as it does right now, as if you'd just had it delivered from the furniture store."

She shouldn't have said that last bit. *She knew she shouldn't have said it.* Speaking her mind was just *one* of her many flaws.

"If it isn't in my head, it's not important," he stated bluntly, reading her thoughts with humiliating accuracy. "The clutter I leave to my secretary's discretion." His low voice rumbled through her body.

If the truth be known, clutter was Sam's middle name. She'd lived with it all her life. In an office like this, where everything was in perfect order and spotless, she'd go crazy. In fact, she would have said so if he'd been anyone else except the man who could get her fired.

"Do you recall emptying the wastebasket?" he demanded in a decidedly chilly tone.

She lifted her rounded chin a little higher. "I would have done, but there was nothing in it."

His lips twisted unpleasantly. No doubt he thought she was being impudent again. Clearly not satisfied with her answers, he buzzed his secretary. "Please come inside, Mrs. Athas, and bring your notepad with you."

Seconds later, the woman who dealt on a daily basis with his billion-dollar clutter, entered his inner sanctum.

She was carrying the small notepad in her hand. It's yellow color triggered a memory.

Sam groaned, alerting her interrogator.

"You were about to say something?" he prodded, a merciless gleam entering those black depths.

"I—I remember now," she stammered. "I did see a yellow piece of notepaper, but it was on the floor next to the wastebasket. I assumed someone had aimed for it, but had missed..."

The inference didn't escape him and his lips thinned, making her quiver inwardly. "Since it was exactly what I needed, I—" She looked everywhere except at him. "I put it in my pocket."

By now his hands were on his hips. To her consternation, his secretary had conveniently disappeared. Sam took this as the worst of omens.

He muttered several epithets not worthy of repeating before he demanded, "Explain to me why you would have confiscated a supposed piece of refuse from my private office."

His arrogance was too much!

"Actually, there's a perfectly good reason," she fired back, cognizant of heat building in her cheeks.

"For your sake, there'd better be," he stated with more than a hint of underlying menace.

Sam didn't like to be threatened. Staring him down she began, "I was vacuuming the carpet beneath your desk when I saw the exact piece of paper I needed to finish my collage."

"Collage?" he bit out.

"My senior art project," she defended boldly because she was on steady ground. "At the beginning of this semester my professor, Dr. Giddings, insisted that we could only use those bits of paper left on the grass, the ground, the sidewalk or the floor. No cheating by dipping into garbage receptacles, no using scissors to alter shape. Everything had to go into the collage as found.''

Warming to her subject she blurted, ''With the exception of newspapers, telephone directories or cardboard, we could use absolutely anything else made of paper. The whole idea of the project was to be as original as possible, and still create an interesting design worthy of hanging in an art gallery.''

Not stopping for breath she explained, ''When Dr. Giddings first gave us the assignment, I didn't realize how fun, how challenging this final project would be. For weeks I've been walking around the city with my eyes on the ground, and I've come up with the most amazing finds which are now attached to my canvas.''

By now *his* eyes had become black slits. ''So you're telling me that the note my secretary left on this desk is now a part of *your* collage?''

''Yes. But I didn't take it from your desk. She must have created a draft and inadvertently knocked it to the floor without realizing it.''

While Sam spoke, he raked a bronzed hand through vibrant, ebony hair. She longed to twine her fingers in it, and the distraction made it practically impossible for her to concentrate.

What was wrong with her? Up to now she'd never become seriously interested in the men who'd wanted a relationship with her. Yet Mr. Kostopoulos, a total stranger, had already ignited a fire in her that was growing stronger with every sparring comment.

''Your explanation is so incredibly absurd, I'm half inclined to believe you're telling me the truth.''

''It's certainly no more absurd than the fact that you have a Picasso hanging on the wall.''

He blinked. ''What does the Picasso have to do with this conversation?''

Obviously he wasn't used to anyone standing up to him. She got a perverse thrill out of shocking him.

"It has everything to do with it. You're an art lover who probably can't paint a straight line." *Mistake number nine or ten. She'd lost count, but it didn't matter. Something about him had made her lose control.*

"Dr. Gidding's is an artist who wouldn't know the first thing about your corporate clutter. The point is, you both love Picasso. While you spend your millions on his art so you can look at it from your comfortable leather chair, my poverty-stricken professor, who probably won't be a legend until long after he has gone, has made us study Picasso and put his credo to the test."

The man confronting her looked incredulous. "What credo?"

"Picasso said, and I quote, 'The artist is a receptacle for emotions that come from all over the place; from the sky, from the earth, from a passing shape, from a spider's web, *from a scrap of paper*. We must pick out what is good for us where we can find it.' End of quote."

He thought she was insane. Right now, she felt that she was...

"Being a disciple of Picasso, Dr. Giddings challenged us to create beauty from the scraps of paper we found."

For an instant their gazes collided, creating a new kind of turmoil in her breast, one that squeezed the air out of her lungs for no good reason.

After an eternity, "Where is this—" He paused. "Work of art?" The mockery in his grating tone was as unmistakable as his derision.

He didn't believe her.

She felt another rush of adrenaline, the kind that prompted her to say things which generally got her into trouble. "At the university."

"Very well. Then we'll drive there and get it."

"I'm afraid that note has already adhered to the wallpaper paste. If I try to pry it loose, my collage will be ruined." To her mortification, the last few words had come out on a wobble. If she had anything to say about it, that art project was her passport to a brilliant future, one she intended to lord in her father's face one day. Sam wasn't about to jeopardize everything she'd worked so hard to achieve. Not for Mr. Kostopoulos, not for anybody!

"Even if I could extricate it, chances are you won't be able to read what was written on it."

She watched the ominous rise and fall of his chest. "Then you'd better start praying that the gods are smiling kindly on you today. I need that number, and there's no point in trying to dissuade me with those sodden eyes."

"Sodden—" she practically shrieked the word.

"Hmm...like drenched blue pansies. I'll warn you now—a woman's tears have no affect on me whatsoever."

She gritted her teeth. "And a man's billions hold no sway with me. You think you're some invincible god who can make mortals tremble with one bellow, and a simple lift of those black eyebrows. Well, I have news for you, Mr. Kofolopogos, or whatever your name is—"

By now her slenderly rounded body had gone rigid. "*This* mortal isn't intimidated. Whoever called and left that number will call again. And if your secretary is so sensational, then she should have taken the number down on one of those pads that makes a copy. The point is, no phone number could possibly be as important as my final grade!"

At her declaration, his features froze. "Since you know absolutely nothing about my life except what you glean from the gossips in this building, I'll let that comment pass."

Unfortunately the truth of his remark deepened the fiery red of her cheeks. But it was the bleakness of his rebuke which sent an icy shiver through her body, taking some of the fight out of her, warning her not to antagonize him any further.

"Look Mr. Kostopoulos— I'm sorry I lost my temper. I'm sorry this whole thing has happened. But you have to know it wasn't intentional. The trouble is, I'm not sure if my professor is still there. It's the weekend. Everything could be locked up until Monday."

"Then I'll find someone to let us in, or call your professor myself."

"But—"

"Shall we go?"

He ignored her distress and strode toward the doors leading to his private elevator. It was smaller than the ones built for public access. Next to his six foot three frame, she felt minuscule. He pushed a button and the door closed.

Like Persephone being spirited to the underworld by the merciless god, Hades, Mr. Kostopoulos plummeted them the sixty-plus floors to the car park below ground. Throughout the swift descent, her arm brushed against his, making her unbearably aware of his hard, powerful body, the faint, clean smell of the soap he used combined with his own male scent.

As far as she was concerned, he was the antithesis of her artistic, mostly bearded male friends who were generally undernourished, impoverished, and most importantly, benign.

This man projected an aura of physical and mental strength which came from facing life head-on, and enjoying every dangerous second of it.

She imagined he daunted the most self-confident male. That quality alone made him an exceptional man, one she secretly admired.

Without question his impact on the opposite sex was equally profound. Sam would be a liar if she didn't admit he had a disturbing, earthy appeal.

Instinctively she felt that the forbidding Mr. Kostopoulos was a unique mortal who created his own destiny. She'd never met anyone remotely like him. Though loathe to admit it, he excited her in a frightening kind of way. That phone number had to be of life-and-death importance for him to go to these extremes. Something told her it had nothing to do with business.

Out of a sense of self-preservation, she purposely held herself rigid so they wouldn't touch. In the close confines of the elevator, she didn't want him picking up on any more of her private thoughts. The head of a world-wide conglomerate didn't get to be that way without possessing the unnerving capacity to gauge the weakness of an individual and use that knowledge to the utmost advantage.

Upon exiting the private elevator, a mustached man from the garage had parked a black Mercedes sedan in the alley in front of the doors. He stepped forward and helped Sam into the passenger seat of the car while Mr. Kostopoulos walked around and got behind the wheel.

The two men conversed in what was undoubtedly Greek. It all sounded foreign and mysterious. Sam had taken Spanish in high school and French in college, but anything outside the Romance languages was anathema to her.

When the other man laughed, Sam cringed. She feared that her abductor was regaling his employee about the wild story she'd concocted.

Clearly Mr. Kostopoulos wouldn't believe her until he had the note back in hand. Thank heaven she'd been honest with him and could prove it. Still, she didn't like being talked about behind her back.

Once they'd cleared the drive and merged with the

horrific city traffic, a deep voice murmured, "Relax, *thespinis*. George was confiding his little son's latest antics. Your guilty secrets are still safe."

Good grief. He knew everything she was thinking. Was her face that transparent?

"For the time being," he continued in the same vein, "all I require is that you be my navigator. Keep in mind that I have an appointment at four-thirty."

She fiddled with the hem of her denim shirt. "I'll keep it in mind, but I can't do anything about heavy traffic, or the possibility that the art department may be closed. You'll need to go left at the next corner."

He lounged back in the seat, negotiating lane changes with the expertise of a New York City cabdriver. "If you're leading me on a wild-goose chase, be assured that you will find yourself out of work before evening."

Sam bristled. "Since I'm down to the last hundred dollars in my checking account, it hardly stands to reason that I would do anything to jeopardize my job at Manhattan Cleaners.

"Of course, that's something you would never understand," she complained to herself, but he heard her. Mocking laughter unexpectedly rumbled out of him, making her body tingle.

"You think I don't remember what it was like for a destitute, barefooted boy on Serifos who was forced to scrounge for jobs no one else would do, only to be given a few pitiful *drachma* a day?"

There was such a wealth of emotion underlying his revelation, it took her a moment to realize he'd just given her a glimpse of the man behind his wealthy, sophisticated veneer. Unless of course he was trying to arouse her compassion. *He was doing a wonderful job of it, but she wasn't about to let him get to her any more.*

"I recall reading the very same thing about Aristotle Onassis," she taunted.

"Our beginnings are not so dissimilar," was all he deigned to say.

Like most foolish people, Sam had made assumptions that Mr. Kostopoulos had been born to wealth, and had learned how to play with his inheritance, aggrandizing his unearned fortune in astronomical ways.

The fact that a dirt-poor young Greek boy had risen to Olympian heights on sheer grit and determination made him a much more devastating adversary, one she couldn't help but admire despite his autocratic manner.

Sam found herself wanting to know more about him, but was in no position to be asking him questions. What little she'd heard about him had been gleaned from gossip in newspapers and magazines, and the people who worked in the building.

After meeting him in person, he was even more enigmatic than the journalists made him out to be. He was also more attractive, and he drove too fast for her peace of mind.

She had the strongest suspicion that his business headquarters in Athens—where the traffic was purported to be the worst—had everything to do with the fact that they'd arrived at the university in half the time it would have taken her, if she'd had a car.

He turned into a section reserved for faculty parking and pulled to a stop in the first available space.

"They tow away cars without permits," she warned him.

"George can always come for us in the limo. Right now the only thing of importance is that note. Let's go."

Sam almost had to run to keep up with him. The second they entered the building, she breathed a sigh of relief to discover that Dr. Giddings's secretary hadn't gone home yet.

"Lois?"

The older woman lifted her head. "Hi, Sam. What are you doing back here?"

Lois was trying hard, but she couldn't keep her eyes from straying to the imposing dark figure dominating the cubbyhole which served as the art department's office. *Who could blame her*?

Under other less precarious circumstances, Sam would have introduced them. Finding out he was *the* Kostopoulos of Kostopoulos Shipping would have made Lois's year. But because Sam hated the limelight, and sensed instinctively that her abductor hated it, too, she decided against divulging his identity.

"I need to get my collage back."

"You've got to be kidding! There must be over a hundred of them propped around the gallery. I've already locked it and am ready to go home. This has been a killer day."

"You can say that again. Lois," Sam whispered, "this is an emergency. I don't have time to explain the details right now, but I can't leave here without it."

"Dr. Giddings won't accept late work, Sam."

"It wasn't late. You logged it in yourself! It's just that I'm in terrible trouble and have to fix something on it. I'll bring it back first thing Monday morning. He'll never know. If you'll do this favor for me, I'll give you that tablecloth I made last semester."

Lois's eyes rounded. "You told me you'd never part with it."

Sam darted Mr. Kostopoulos a covert glance. "I—I changed my mind."

Lois followed Sam's gaze. Lowering her voice she said, "Holy moly. You've been holding out on me. He's incredible. I mean downright, knock-me-dead fantastic. Where on this overcrowded planet did you find *him*?"

"At my night job. Lois, please help me."

"You really want your collage back that badly?"

"Yes. It's a matter of life and death." Which wasn't exactly a lie. In fact, Sam had the distinct feeling her life wouldn't be worth the sum total of the scraps of paper stuck to her canvas if she couldn't produce the desired note.

The bemused secretary sighed aloud and pulled a key out of the drawer. "All right. Go on in and get it."

"Thank you!" Sam leaned over the counter and gave her a hug. "He's going to help me look for it, so it shouldn't take too long."

With key in hand, Sam hurried down the hall, beckoning Mr. Kostopoulos to follow.

"What exactly are we looking for?" His deep voice reverberated in the darkness. She felt for the light switch on the wall, her heart thudding painfully. His nearness was starting to affect her that way, and the fear that she wouldn't be able to pry the note loose without tearing *it* and the phone number to shreds.

"I-if I've done a halfway decent job, you shouldn't have any trouble spotting it."

"Is this a riddle of some kind?"

"Not exactly. It's just that I'm hoping it will leap out at you."

On that note, she found the switch which illuminated the gallery. Collages of every design and color, from white to psychedelic, filled the room, leaving little space to maneuver. Each one had to be three feet by four feet, therefore the unity of shape didn't make their task any easier.

While she took in the enormity of the project facing them, a pair of unfathomable black eyes impaled her.

"I can already see a dozen projects which are fairly blinding me at the moment," he growled with heavy sarcasm.

An imp of mischief not unmingled with fear made her

want to prolong the moment of truth until the last second, but she supposed her last second was up.

"I'll give you a hint. Mine will probably be the only one which will speak to you personally. That is—" Her voice caught, "if—as I mentioned earlier—I've accomplished my objective."

His expression darkened. "We're running out of time, Ms. Telford."

"All right. I decided to create a collage of your office building."

CHAPTER TWO

"WHAT do you mean, my office building?"

"Yours is the most beautiful one in the city, all-gleaming cream with a royal blue motif. Since I work there every night, I decided to use it as the subject of my project. But I've filled it with people so it won't look so lonely."

One brow descended. "Lonely?"

"Yes." By now she was busy looking for her design. "All buildings have an essence. Yours reminds me of a fabulous Greek temple, magnificent, but a little remote. I put people in all the windows to make it a happier place."

Once again her tongue had run away with her.

But now that she'd met him, she understood why she'd felt those emotions. Like his building, he was aloof, yet magnificent. *He was wonderful*, in a scary, exciting kind of way.

When she discovered him staring at her with a strange look in his eyes, she hurriedly bent to her task, trying to pretend she was alone, but it was impossible to forget he was in the room with her.

Every so often she found herself casting him a furtive glance. He appeared to be studying each work of art with more than cursory interest. It shouldn't have surprised her. A true art lover like himself could never remain indifferent, no matter the form. Many of the collages were bizarre, but she'd glimpsed a few which were true *chefs d'oeuvres*. Apparently he thought so, too.

Maybe she was a little nobody of no significance. But how she hoped he'd at least find her artwork outstanding.

Then she chastised herself for speculating about foolish dreams when she knew his only interest was in getting the phone number off that yellow piece of paper.

What if it couldn't be done? What if she couldn't perform the required miracle?

Another five minutes passed as they continued to sift through the various canvases. Sam was beginning to wonder if her project was even in there when she heard Mr. Kostopoulos make a sound underneath his breath.

Her head jerked around in time to see him pluck one of the projects from a stack and hold it in front of him.

A smothered imprecation escaped his lips. "You made *this* with discarded pieces of paper?" His incredulity gave her no clue as to whether he liked her effort or not.

In a small voice she answered, "Yes."

There was an uncomfortable silence. Then, "Where's my note?"

Sam supposed the gruffness in his tone was to be expected. After all, she *had* taken it from his private office, even if she'd found it on the floor.

"It's in the top right window."

By this time she'd come to stand next to him, and pointed it out with a trembling finger. She could feel his gaze studying her with a thoroughness that left her shaken.

"That's *my* office."

"I—I had no idea," she defended. "But I'll admit it's an odd coincidence."

"Is it?" he challenged.

Thank heaven Lois chose that moment to poke her head inside the gallery. "Have you found your project yet? I'm closing up now."

"Y-yes," Sam stammered. "We're coming. Thanks, Lois. I owe you."

"Just remember to get it back here before eight

Monday morning. I've seen Dr. Giddings hold up some-one's graduation for much less.''

"You're graduating?'' Mr. Kostopoulos demanded when they had left the building and were once more ensconced in his car with the collage safely deposited in the trunk.

Sam averted her eyes from his striking features. "A week from yesterday. But you heard Lois. If my profes-sor finds out what I've done, I'll have to take the class over again to graduate. In any event, the damage will cost me a drop in grade.''

"Let's not worry about that right now. If the worst happens, I'll explain the circumstances to your profes-sor.''

She shook her head. "Once he's made up his mind, I doubt even you could sway Dr. Giddings.''

"We'll see,'' was all he condescended to say until they'd retraced their steps and had come in sight of his office building. That's when she started to panic. He was expecting results she couldn't promise to produce.

"Mr. Kostopoulos—I need special tools and am going to have to go to my apartment. If you'll drop me off there, you can keep your appointment. I'll phone you when I've finished.''

"What is your address?''

Pleased he was so amenable to the suggestion, she gave him directions, then sat back in relief because they'd be parting company shortly.

She would never be able to work with him standing over her shoulder. Not only was she nervous about the outcome, she was too aware of him on a physical level to pretend indifference to his presence.

"Turn left at the next light. My apartment is on the south, in the middle of the block. The traffic is so bad you'd better just let me out on the corner.''

As he slowed for the light, she reached for the door

handle, but the catch didn't give. Her head whipped around. "Will you please undo the lock?"

Her request fell on deaf ears because he had pulled a cellular phone from the inside of his suit jacket and was telling his secretary to reschedule his appointment for the following week.

Suddenly Sam's heart began to race because she had this horrible premonition that he intended to come up to her apartment and watch her perform the required surgery.

There were several reasons why she couldn't allow him over her threshold. For one thing, her one-bedroom apartment was in complete chaos. For another, there simply wasn't enough room inside for both of them. The kitchen and living area were combined. The only place he'd be able to sit down was the couch, and it would take her five minutes just to clear a space for him.

She started to tell him he couldn't park in the zone marked for trucks making deliveries, then realized it was pointless. A man like Mr. Kostopoulos wrote his own rules.

By the time she was freed from the confines of the car, he'd removed her collage from the trunk and had preceded her to the front doors of the building.

Once inside the outer lobby, she punched in the code which gave access to the elevator entrance. Already she was feeling claustrophobic.

Taking a deep breath she said, "It won't be necessary for you to come all the way up. If you'll give me a number where you can be reached, I'll call you the second I've finished."

The elevator door opened and he ushered her inside. His dark eyes swept over her once more. "I'm already in the neighborhood. There's no point in my leaving until I get what I came for."

At that remark, they rode the rest of the way to the

seventh floor in silence. He followed at her heel until they came to her apartment three doors down the hall.

Before she could bring herself to unlock it, she turned to him, slightly out of breath. "Perhaps it would be better if you waited in your car."

His brows furrowed. "If you're worried what your lover will think, I'll be happy to explain why your privacy is being invaded."

Heat swarmed her cheeks. "There isn't enough room for me, let alone anyone else."

He gave a negligent shrug of his powerful shoulders. "Then I don't see the problem. My childhood was spent in a room not much larger than a closet. It's nothing to be ashamed of."

She clenched her teeth. "Did it ever occur to you that I'm not ready for company?"

"I'm not company," he retorted with maddening *non chalance*. "Come. Give me the key."

In the next instance he'd removed it from her rigid fingers and had opened the door, signaling that she should precede him.

That brief contact of skin against skin sent a quickening through her body she'd never experienced before. The sensation electrified her, confusing her on too many levels.

"Where shall I put this so you can get started?"

The bland question indicated that he hadn't been fazed by the brush of their fingers. She berated herself for reacting so foolishly, and marched over to the card table where she whisked away some orange peels, the visible remains of a breakfast hastily swallowed earlier that day.

Without apology she muttered, "You can put it down here."

Of necessity, he had to follow in her footsteps, stepping over not only her hair dryer, but the spray-stained newspaper still spread on the floor.

Last night she'd given her project a final protective coating, but because of the inclement weather, her apartment had felt more humid than usual. She was so afraid the collage wouldn't dry out, she'd gotten up in the early hours of the morning to speed the process by using her hair dryer.

"I'll look for my hammer and chisel."

Along with most of her other art supplies, she'd put the tools from her sculpture class in the tiny linen cupboard next to the bathroom. But since her sophomore year, she'd stored a lot of dyes and acrylics there, as well. It took some doing to find what she needed, and she ended up putting everything on the floor to be cleaned up later.

When she returned to the living room-cum-kitchen with her tools and put them on the card table, she found Mr. Kostopoulos perched on the arm of the couch studying the latest tablecloth she'd created. It was one to which she'd applied a hot wax design, then dyed, before draping across her secondhand couch to dry out.

With nowhere to pace in her postage stamp dwelling, he'd had little alternative but to plant himself there, unless he'd wanted to remain standing.

Suddenly she saw something clasped in his left hand. To her horror it turned out to be her rolling pin which she used for everything under the sun except cooking.

For the first time since meeting him, she thought she detected a tiny flicker of mirth in the black recesses of his eyes. He held up the well-worn kitchen utensil whose roller contained so many dents it resembled the surface of the moon. "I presume you keep this handy in case of intruders."

She blinked. Until he'd mentioned it, she hadn't thought of using her rolling pin as a weapon. "What a wonderful idea!"

Her spontaneity must have amused him because his

lips twitched ever so slightly, a feat she hadn't thought possible.

"Actually, I used it to create my collage."

In a level tone he murmured, "Go on."

"You want me to explain?"

"Yes, Ms. Telford. I can't remember the last time I was this entertained by another human being."

His comment could be taken in a variety of ways, all of them less than gratifying or complimentary.

In another aside he added, "I'm fascinated to discover how this instrument contributed to the final product."

Did he even like the final product? He still hadn't said a word about it.

"If you really want to know, I'll demonstrate."

Without meeting his penetrating gaze, she took the rolling pin from his hand, then tore off a corner of the newspaper lying on the floor.

She could sense his body next to hers as she wadded the paper in her palm, then cleared a glass and some cutlery from her minuscule counter so she'd have room to work. Placing the little wad in the center, she began pressing it down with the roller. She ran over it this way, then that.

"You have to do this about ten times until you achieve the desired crinkled effect. I did this to every piece of paper in the collage so that each one resembled an old man's weathered face. Then I opened the paper and applied a hair spray meant to add lighter streaks to dull blond hair. Every tiny crease captured the glaze, gilding it, producing an all-over effect not unlike *faience*, a kind of fine porcelain with thousands of weblike lines.

"After the piece dried, I cupped it in my palm, shaping it to resemble people or the Greek motif on the outside of your building. Then I curled the ends under, and dipped them in wallpaper paste before working the treated paper into the collage.

"As you can see—" Her eyes darted to the canvas propped on the card table. "The spray enhanced every color, but more importantly, the overall impression should convince the viewer that he's looking at a collage made of the most translucent bone china." After a slight pause, "At least, it's *supposed* to create that effect."

"Rest assured you achieved your goal. In fact, you achieved a great deal more than that," came the cryptic comment. As he said the words, his dark gaze trapped her astonished one, sending a strange thrill of sensation chasing across her skin.

Unused to the hairs standing on the back of her neck, she rushed over to the card table to begin her task.

Out of the periphery, she watched him approach her only folding chair and examine the half dozen remnants of upholstery cloth she'd hand woven before he fingered various fishnet chains she'd designed. They were hanging from the ceiling in one corner of the room.

While he was thus engrossed, she laid the canvas flat on the tabletop. Using her hip for leverage, she positioned it against the wall. Carefully she placed the edge of the chisel at the base of the window in the collage and started to tap the handle with the hammer.

But she hadn't counted on the card table jiggling under the pressure.

It caused the canvas to slide, which in turn sent the sharp end of the chisel into the fleshy portion of her palm. Unknowingly she cried out as blood gushed all over her artwork.

She had no idea anyone of Mr. Kostopoulos's size could move as fast as he did. In a lightning gesture he'd pulled a snowy white handkerchief from his pocket and had grabbed her hand to stop the bleeding.

Oblivious to the pain, her heart began to thud from the close proximity of their bodies. She heard him mutter another unrepeatable epithet. "The wound is too deep to close by itself. You're going to need stitches and a tetanus shot.''

"I'll be all right," she murmured breathily. For some reason, the sight of blood always made her feel faint. She had to fight the urge to cling to him and draw from his strength. "I don't have any insurance and can't afford a visit to the doctor.''

"You think I'd let you pay when I was the one who forced the issue?" His scathing tone left her in little doubt he was taking full responsibility. "We're leaving for my doctor *now*."

"But my collage! I've got to get the blood off it.''

No sooner had she spoken those words than he relinquished his hold of her hand and took her canvas to the sink to run cold water over the soiled portion. Within seconds it looked like new again. In a deft movement, he propped it on the card table, much the same way she'd done the night before.

Immediately his concerned gaze flicked to her injured hand where she pressed the handkerchief to apply pressure.

"It's to your credit that you had the foresight to spray the collage with a protective sealer. Otherwise the water would have permeated the paper and ruined your unique masterpiece. Now that we've erased that worry, we can go.''

His compliment, albeit grudgingly given, filled her with such warmth, she went along without protest.

Unbelievably, she found herself back in his car where a new, strange silence prevailed. He seemed to be in a world all his own. For that matter, so was she. The events of the last few hours had left her bemused and shaken.

As soon as they merged with the traffic, he managed to get her to a private clinic in record time.

Of course the receptionist knew him on sight, and

though there were still some patients in the waiting area, one word from him and Sam was rushed into the first available examining room.

Apparently Dr. Strike was a compatriot of her abductor. The second the attractive, dark-haired man breezed inside, his face broke out in a broad smile. "*Perseus*!" he called to Mr. Kostopoulos, and they began conversing in Greek like longtime friends.

Sam sat there in stunned surprise. The image of the god Hades faded from her mind as she remembered her favorite story from Greek mythology.

The strong, handsome Perseus, son of Zeus and Danae, rejected by his mother's abductor, the cunning King Polydectes, set out to prove he could do anything, even free his mother, and eventually brought home not only the head of Medusa to turn the king and his courtiers to stone, but acquired a wife in the form of the beautiful Andromeda whom he rescued from the sea monster.

It may have been a coincidence, but to a large degree, Mr. Kostopoulos's life appeared to have paralleled that of the mythical Perseus. As today's world viewed him, Perseus Kostopoulos was a presence to reckon with. Even Sam had attributed him with godlike characteristics the first moment she'd laid eyes on him.

Were there more similarities? Was he on a quest of some kind? Was there still a woman to be rescued whom he'd make his own?

For an unknown reason, those fanciful thoughts were very disturbing to Sam who could wish *she* were that special woman he'd been roaming the world to find.

Realizing what dangerous channels her thoughts were drifting into, she made a determined effort to concentrate on the doctor's instructions as he put in three stitches, bound her hand with gauze and gave her a tetanus shot. All the while he spoke, she felt his speculative gaze.

Naturally he was trying to work out why someone of Perseus Kostopoulos's stature would be in the company of an insignificant college student like herself.

Though too discreet to be obvious, Sam sensed the doctor's curiosity which, oddly enough, her companion hadn't satisfied. Apparently he wished to keep the particulars of their association to himself.

As soon as she thanked Dr. Strike for fitting her in so fast, she felt Perseus's hand at her elbow to usher her out of the clinic. Already he'd taken on the persona of the strong and brave Greek god in her mind, and she no longer thought of him as Mr. Kostopoulos.

With a sense of *déjà vu* they returned to her apartment where he submitted her to more toe-curling scrutiny. "While you obey doctor's orders and keep your hand elevated, I'll fix you something to drink and get to work."

Actually, she felt too weak to argue with him. Deep inside she knew her injury played only a minor part in what was really ailing her, but she'd rather die than allow him to discern the truth—that his presence was wreaking havoc with her emotions.

As an unfamiliar lethargy depleted her energy, she removed the tablecloth from the couch and sank down in one corner, content to watch *him* for a change. In a few hours she'd have to report to her night job and didn't know how she was going to make it to the front door, let alone walk the eight blocks in the warm May drizzle.

"There's some tea in the cupboard over the stove."

As if he were used to this, he shed his suit jacket and tie, rolled up his shirt sleeves and boiled some water. Through half-closed eyes she watched him maneuver in the tiny space, obviously no stranger to mundane tasks when necessity dictated.

Though he dwarfed her apartment, she had to admit she liked his solid male presence, and didn't mind the invasion as much as she'd supposed.

Despite their cajolings, no other man had ever made it past her front door. Perseus, on the other hand, had simply removed the key from her trembling fingers and taken over her apartment and her life. *And you let him Sam, because you couldn't help yourself. You still can't...*

Her head fell back against the couch. She had to admit that for a little while it felt good to be waited on. So good, in fact, she almost forgot the reason for his unexpected entry into her life. That is until he handed her a cup of hot tea before going to work on her collage.

He seemed to know exactly what he was about. When he bent over to dislodge the note with her tools, she noticed the play of muscle across his shoulders, the strength of his rugged physique. If she were into drawing human figures, he'd make a perfect model in all his raw, male splendor.

Once more upset at the direction of her uncontrollable thoughts, she drank her tea thirstily. He'd made it strong, and had added more sugar than she generally used. Her mouth curved upward. Greeks had a noted penchant for sweets. She guessed he was no exception.

"I've worked it loose," his deep voice announced with satisfaction. "What's the next step?"

Totally engrossed in thoughts of his likes and dislikes, she didn't realize until too late that he'd caught her staring at him. This time prickly heat washed over her entire body, even to the roots of her abundant gold hair.

Quickly averting her eyes she murmured, "I intended to use a solvent to loosen the paste and soften the paper enough to open it. Just a moment and I'll get it."

"Tell me where it is and I'll find it."

The authority in his tone warned her that if she tried

to get up, he'd use his daunting physical strength to prevent her from leaving the couch.

Faced with the knowledge that he'd have to get into her bedroom closet to locate the solvent, she didn't know which alternative was the most unpalatable. Especially considering that her more intimate apparel and nightware hung from hooks on the door.

Of course a woman's underclothing would hold no mystery for a man like Perseus Kostopoulos, but it wouldn't be just any woman's undergarments practically hitting him in the face. They would be *hers*.

Perhaps most women didn't care, but she'd never grown up with a father or brothers. Since her morals prevented her from having an intimate relationship with a man outside of marriage, she'd been very selective about the men she had allowed in her life.

To date she'd only had one semiserious boyfriend. When he found out she expected marriage before going to bed with him, he accused her of being an outdated prude, and he moved on to someone else. That was just fine with her. She preferred her solitary existence, and hadn't counted on an unknown entity like Perseus knocking the foundations out from under her.

"Why the hesitation?" he mocked, seemingly as amused by her reticence as he was irritated.

She closed her eyes in defeat and lay back against the cushion with her hand propped upright. "I-it's in a box on the closet floor in the bedroom."

He'd disappeared before she had the courage to open them again. Several minutes passed by with no sign of him. When he didn't come back out, she started to grow nervous and got off the couch to investigate.

Revived by the tea, she didn't feel as unsteady as before and hurriedly made her way to the bedroom.

"The box is in plain—" But the rest of the words never came out of her mouth. He had virtually emptied the contents of her closet. Not the stuff on the shelves or floor, but everything on hangers, mainly samples of fabrics she'd been designing since her early teens.

In actuality, the contents bore more resemblance to the materials of an upholstery department in a furniture store than they did a woman's wardrobe. The few ancient skirts and blouses she possessed had been shoved into one corner.

He'd laid out the large samples across her unmade twin bed. Some were woven, others were hand-painted or stenciled. He didn't even bother to lift his head to acknowledge her presence, let alone apologize for the liberty he'd taken.

"Where did you get these?" he asked in that low, vibrant voice she'd be able to recognize out of a thousand others.

"I made them."

His dark head reared back, and he sent her a piercing glance she couldn't decipher. "If that's true, then you have a touch of genius in you."

"You think?" Her words came out more like a squeak.

"You mean you don't know?" He actually sounded angry.

Inordinately pleased by the compliment, she forgot to be mad and smiled at him. For Perseus Kostopoulos, a known art lover and head of one of the world's most prestigious textile companies, to give her such an unsolicited accolade, gave her hope that she wasn't wasting her time completely.

Over the years Sam had received compliments on her work from her peers, but for some reason, she'd never elicited praise from her professors.

There had been times when she'd been tempted to tell them she was Jules Gregory's daughter, in order to evoke even a little recognition. But pride had always held her back. If she couldn't succeed on her own, then she refused to trade on her father's name.

As far as Sam was concerned, he was a despicable man who couldn't have cared less that her mother had passed away, or that his daughter had been left on her own.

Swallowing her bitterness, Sam leaned over to get the solvent, then headed for the kitchen. Perseus followed her and took the can from her hand to open the lid. Again she felt the brush of his skin with a sense of wonder and trembling.

Refusing to meet his eyes which had been studying her since her flight from the bedroom, she rummaged for a dish in the cupboard. "If your secretary wrote the number in pen, the solvent won't destroy it. Unfortunately, I'm afraid it might wash out any notations made by pencil."

"She uses both," he muttered, before pouring some liquid into the bowl she handed him. "That's the chance we'll have to take." So saying, he put the crumpled piece of yellow paper in the liquid. "How long shall I leave it in?"

Her injured hand had started to throb. Worse, she could feel a headache coming on, probably because this wasn't going to work, and then he'd leave and she'd never see him again.

The idea that he might be walking out of her life in a few minutes was enough to bring on a migraine, let alone the sense of loss to her heart.

"Give it a minute, then take it out and test it to see how soft it's getting."

He did as she suggested, then shook his head. "It needs more time."

"Leave it another two minutes."

Once again he submerged it.

She watched from a little way off, consumed by curiosity, and the nagging fear that her time alone with him was numbered by precious minutes ticking away far too fast.

Finally, when she couldn't stand it any longer she blurted, "Why is this particular number so important to you?"

His body tautened, making her wish she'd kept silent.

"Twenty years ago my beloved fiancée plunged a knife into my jaw, then disappeared."

His fiancée?

"I've been looking for her ever since."

Sam's musings had been right. He *was* on a quest for the woman who'd undoubtedly marked him in ways that went much deeper than his scar. Sam already hated that woman with a ferocity she couldn't even explain to herself.

"Little by little the field of the search has narrowed," he spoke on, unaware of her uncharitable thoughts toward the woman he loved. "She's grown tired of running from me. Quite the reverse," he muttered grimly. "In fact, my sources indicate she's probably the one who phoned my office leaving her private phone number with Mrs. Athas."

The explanation was so shocking, so different from the picture Sam had in her mind of his being scarred in a street fight, she started to shiver and couldn't stop.

"But if she loved you enough to get engaged, and you loved her—"

His features hardened. "More than life itself. We made our own vows on Delos, at the temple of Apollo."

His admission shouldn't have devastated her. Perseus Kostopoulos couldn't possibly mean anything to her.

But he did…

"Then why—"

"I think this is soft enough now," he broke in without answering her burning question. Something told her she'd heard all she was going to hear.

Sam hadn't been aware of holding her breath until he

unfolded the edges of the yellow note. Her heart plummeted to her feet because the writing was no longer there.

As if he'd suddenly been scalded, he let the paper fall to the counter.

"I'm so sorry," she whispered in anguish. "I—I wish to heaven I'd never cleaned your office."

"It's too late for regrets, Ms. Telford." The words dropped like rocks. "Where is the wallpaper paste? I'll repair the damage to your collage."

"That won't be necessary. I'll do it."

"Not with an injured hand."

Like lightning he disappeared, then returned with the paste which he'd found on the floor in the hall.

In very little time he'd put the missing piece back so that it looked as if it had never been removed. All she would have to do was spray that spot one more time to make it like new.

"Thank you," she murmured, but doubted he'd heard her because he'd retrieved his cellular phone from his suit jacket and was talking to someone in Greek. Undoubtedly he was calling one of his contacts to let them know he'd been unsuccessful in obtaining the phone number.

Any second now he'd leave her apartment and be lost to her forever. She couldn't bear it, but what could she do unless she held him prisoner at gunpoint. The only problem was, she didn't own a gun because she didn't believe in them.

What an irony that this was the first time she'd ever wished to own a firearm. A double irony because she would use it to keep Perseus inside, instead of out.

When he'd finished his conversation, he eyed her intently.

Here it comes. He's about to tell me goodbye, and I'll never be the same again.

CHAPTER THREE

"I'VE canceled my appointment and arranged for our dinner to be delivered."

Sam reeled and held on to the couch back for support. "What?"

"After what I've put you through today, I need to make amends. Furthermore, I'm hungry and wager you are too."

"Well, yes...but—"

"Then it's settled," he cut in without a qualm. "While you obey doctor's orders and rest, I'll clean things up."

"No, please. I can't let you do that."

"You're in no position to stop me. By the way, while we were at the doctor, I contacted Manhattan Cleaners and told them about your injury. The person in charge said you should take off as much time as you needed to heal. I told them you'd get back to them in a few days."

On that succinct note he began tidying the room. Sam sank back on the couch, too bemused by the circumstances to argue. Someone upstairs had heard her, and granted her a few more minutes of Perseus's precious company. But ungrateful wretch that she was, she was greedy. She wanted it to last *forever*.

Unfortunately it was only a short half hour later that she heard a knock on her apartment door, and jerked to a sitting position. But Perseus was faster and had opened it before she could get up from the couch. "*Kalispera, Arianna*," she heard him say.

The dark-haired, middle-aged woman answered, "*Gia sas, Kyrie Kostopoulos*." She was holding a huge sack, yet even from the distance, Sam could detect a delicious aroma filling the room which made her mouth water. She couldn't remember the last time anything had smelled so good.

"*Efcharisto.*"

Except for that last word which she'd figured out meant, "thank you," Sam didn't understand the rest of their conversation before the woman went away again, leaving the two of them alone once more.

"Arianna is the best cook in New York. Tonight we will enjoy mincemeat kebab and baby lamb, roasted with tomato and cheese. For dessert, *galato bouriko*, a sinful custard pastry I promise you'll enjoy."

Sam's eyes widened in surprise as he handed her a heaping plate of food. "Everything looks wonderful."

"It is. But later, when we reach Serifos, and you taste my housekeeper Maria's cooking, then you will know the true meaning of *ambrosia.*"

Her heart did a queer little thump, and the first bite of lamb never reached her mouth. "What do you mean, when *we* reach Serifos?"

He had already made huge inroads into his food. Without meeting her gaze he said, "The gods didn't smile kindly on you after all. Because you stole something from my office that wasn't yours, you must make restitution."

His words were delivered in such a silky tone, it took a second before she understood their thrust.

Here she'd been praying that Perseus wouldn't walk out of her life. Now it seemed she might be granted her wish. But wasn't there an old Spanish proverb somewhere that said, *Beware lest you get what you asked of God*?

She started to grow nervous and lost what little appetite she had.

"It's more than probable that my fiancée, who has

returned to Serifos after a twenty year absence with the sole intent of marrying the heartbroken fiancé of her youth, hoped to reach me by phone and beg my forgiveness before we saw each other again.

"I've decided that I'm glad I couldn't return her call after all. Bringing you back to Serifos as my wife will speak more eloquently than any words I might have said to her.

When all danger has passed, you will be freed to continue with the rest of your life. Be assured, *thespinis*, your nights will be your own. You will only have to act the part of my bride, by day."

Bride by day?

He actually planned to use Sam as a pawn to help him face his adored fiancée? Apparently the woman presented so great a danger to his peace of mind, he'd even used the word with Sam.

At such a ludicrous, preposterous idea, Sam should have been laughing hysterically. Or throwing the kebabs in his face... But neither reaction surfaced. Rather, a strange ache had entered her heart as she watched him absently rubbing an index finger over his scar. She wondered if it still hurt him after all this time...

What kind of a woman was this fiancée who held him in thrall to the point that he'd never remarried or stopping trying to find her, even though she'd done such a horrific thing to him?

Was he truly so frightened he might fall under her spell again, he would turn to a total stranger and marry her in his desperation to combat his beloved's attractions?

Sam couldn't imagine a love like that or comprehend it, and decided she didn't want to know.

But a little voice deep inside called her a liar for not owning up to the truth. Just once in her life, Sam had to admit she'd like to know how it felt to be the sum total of a man's existence.

Liar, the voice whispered again. *Not just any man. Face it, Samantha Telford. You'll probably never see him again, but by some error in the cosmos, Perseus Kostopoulos has crossed your path, and given you the once-in-a-billion chance opportunity to remain in his life for a little longer. As his wife!*

Isn't that what you wanted?

"For a woman who is never without words, your speechless state is extremely gratifying because it means you haven't rejected my decision out of hand. That's good, since the alternative would be that you come live with me, not as my wife, but my pillow friend."

Her cheeks flushed. "You mean, your mistress."

"I would treat you exactly the same way, but I'm afraid the world would not be as charitable to you, if you follow my meaning."

She was very much afraid that she did. Living with Perseus under those conditions would be tantamount to destroying her good name and reputation. Being his wife would be an entirely different proposition.

"Of course to make this more palatable for you, I'm prepared to grant you the three wishes of your heart. You have only to voice them to realize your wildest dreams."

Her eyes narrowed provocatively. She was feeling as capricious and daring as the moment afforded. The corner of her mouth lifted. "My *wildest* dreams?"

It was beyond her wildest imagination—let alone her dreams—to be sitting in her tiny apartment a few feet away from the renowned and breathtaking Perseus Kostopoulos, having just heard him propose marriage to her, no matter his not-so-secret agenda.

"Three wishes, you say?"

A trick of light made his eyes seem even blacker and

more mysterious. "As my closest friends will attest, once made, I never go back on a bargain."

She could believe it.

"Well, that's easy. For one, I've always wished I had enough money to give every deserving, struggling artist at the university a free stipend so he only had to work at one job instead of two or three, in order to afford college."

"*Done*," came the pronouncement, as if from on high. "Since I'd already planned to purchase your art project and have it hung in a place of honor in the foyer of my building, I'll contact Dr. Giddings and establish a perpetual fund in your name which he can administer to needy, deserving art students."

The idea that he planned to buy her collage and put it on display almost made her plate of food fall off her lap onto the couch. But to think what such a monetary gift would mean to impoverished students...

"You'd really do that?" Sam cried out in unabashed astonishment.

"What's your second wish?" he continued in the same vein, completely ignoring her outburst.

He was sitting on the rickety chair he'd carried from the corner and placed opposite the couch, calmly finishing a second helping of lamb.

Her second wish. It was really her first, but at his suggestion, she'd wanted to propose the most outrageous demand she could think of.

Just remembering her hard working, courageous mother made her eyes cloud over. She bit her lip to put a brake on her emotions.

"When Mom died, I didn't have the money to fly her to Cheyenne, Wyoming. She was born there and ought to have been buried in the family plot. I designed a headstone I wanted to have erected to her memory, but it was too costly to have made."

"Done," he came back again in a low, solemn tone.
"Remember that you only have one more wish. It must
be something you want for yourself."

Her third wish.

Sam eyed him covertly. This was only a game.

She had no intention of acting on any of it.

"To have the time and luxury to create beautiful designs for cloth, ceramic tiles and fine-boned china which
other people will clamor to buy."

"Done."

In a lithe move, he rose to his full height and relieved
her of the food she'd barely tasted.

He took everything to the sink, then said over his
broad shoulder, "At my villa on Serifos, there's a whole
wing you can devote to your work. Cottage industries in
the Cyclades have always been the secret of my financial
success.

"Frankly, it's been many years since I've seen designs and patterns as fresh and exciting as yours.
Through my marketing experts, you'll make a small fortune. By the time I've granted you your freedom, you'll
be launched and successful, and you'll never have another money worry again."

While she sat there in a complete stupor, he suddenly
turned and gave her his undivided attention. "I sense
there's a fourth. Tonight I'm in a benevolent-enough
mood to indulge your slightest whim."

*He wanted protection from his fiancée at any cost,
even to binding himself to a temporary wife he didn't
love.*

All along, Sam had been right about him. He had re-
markably sensitivity and a superior intellect which could
ferret out a person's most closely guarded secrets without even trying. His perception was positively scary.

Deep, deep down inside that core of her being, she'd
been waiting for the day when she shouted at her father

that she and her mother had made an even greater success of their lives than he had—*without his acknowledgment or help*—then walk proudly away and *never* look back.

Perseus Kostopoulos was the only god-like mortal who could actually help her achieve that dream before she was old and gray—*and somehow he knew it*, even if she hadn't told him the particulars.

"I—I don't know." She tried to sound unaffected, but was failing miserably. "I'll have to think about it."

"Do that. I'll be back at ten tonight." He took her door key from the kitchen counter and let himself out of the apartment without waiting for a response.

What a clever man to leave her alone so she could contemplate the rest of her life without him.

Before she'd left her apartment earlier in the day to make the walk to his office in the rain, she'd given little thought to a love interest in her life because she'd been too busy getting ready to graduate, too busy to start making her way in the world.

That was before she'd met Perseus Kostopoulos.

Now his stamp was all over her lonely, claustrophobic apartment, from the bedroom to the kitchen sink.

She eyed the gauze bandage wrapped around her hand, evidence of the care she'd received from his own, personal doctor. Her arm ached from the tetanus shot she'd been given, further evidence of that concern.

Sumptuous Greek food he'd had specially prepared for her still sat on the plate waiting to be eaten. Her violated collage, one he planned to buy and place in his office building for the whole world to see, sat propped on the card table, expertly repaired by his capable hands.

Strong, masculine hands which had caught hers to stop the bleeding. Hands she secretly longed to feel in her hair, on her body. Until now, she'd never had such an erotic thought in her life.

It came to her like a revelation that she had fallen in love with Perseus on sight. She didn't care what other people would say about such an absurd, ridiculous statement only hours after having met him.

She couldn't help it. Something told her that if she couldn't have his love, body and soul, for the rest of her life, then she wouldn't want any other man's.

Her mother had said the same thing about her father. She'd loved Jules Gregory from the moment she'd first laid eyes on him. Like mother, like daughter.

Since the possibility of Perseus returning her love was nonexistent, could she be content with the proverbial *half loaf?*

At least she'd have a chance to be close to him for as long as he allowed it. Maybe he'd need to keep her at his side for a long, long time. Long enough to thwart his fiancée. Long enough for him to turn to Sa—

Stop it, Sam. You're being delusional.

If you agree to his proposal, you can never let him know the real reason why you're willing to enter into something which can only cause yourself pain and heartache in the end.

The problem was, she was already experiencing those searing emotions, and he'd only been gone twenty minutes. She couldn't abide the thought of his never coming back...

Though she tried to stay busy straightening her apartment, and still keep her injured hand raised, the next hour passed with agonizing slowness.

By five after ten, she'd worked herself up to a crisis state thinking that maybe he wasn't going to come back, that he'd only been playing with her emotions as final punishment for removing the note from his office in the first place.

When the front door buzzer rang at ten-fifteen, she

was convinced it had to be the building super who was probably returning the key Perseus had taken.

Before she could reach the door, it opened, and Perseus let himself inside, shutting it again. She was *too* happy to see him, and had to avert her eyes so he wouldn't guess how she felt.

"I got caught in traffic. Have you made your decision?" he asked in his deep voice.

Her softly rounded chin lifted. "I wouldn't dream of holding you to my first two wishes, but I do need to get started on a career as soon as possible. Naturally I'd want to prove myself to the person who interviews me, but if you could arrange for a first meeting with the head of personnel of your textile company, that's all I would ask. In return for that favor, I—I'll marry you for a temporary period, Mr. Kostopoulos."

"Perseus," he fired back. "I expect you to use it from here on out."

He murmured something else in his native tongue which needed no translation. The triumphant glitter in those black orbs said it all, bringing her out of the spell he'd cast over her.

Her body quivered in terrified reaction. *What had she done?*

"Where will your graduation take place?"

Her mouth had gone dry. "At Washington Square Park next Friday."

"Are your tests over?"

"Yes."

"Good. Then we'll be married the next day. You'll have to give your notice to Manhattan Cleaners. In the meantime, we'll purchase you a wardrobe and wedding dress. We'll also arrange to have your furnishings packed, and put into storage.

"If you'll tell me where your mother's body is interred, I'll deal with everything so we can take her body back to Wyoming on the company plane after our wedding.

"Once we arrive in Cheyenne, we'll buy the stone you had in mind for your mother's grave and have it made according to your design. When it's finished we'll give her a proper burial, and have the stone put in place before we leave for Athens, which should be about two weeks from now. After we're settled on Serifos, you can send out wedding announcements to anyone you want."

Sam stood there thunderstruck. He'd touched on so many issues, she couldn't compute them all. What made the greatest impression on her mind was his incredible generosity and determination to see her wishes fulfilled where her mother was concerned.

As for everything else, he'd rendered her breathless by the speed with which his mind had worked out every detail. No wonder he was held in awe by the international business community. In a matter of seconds, he'd mapped out their entire life, leaving no stone unturned. All she could do was nod her head in acquiescence.

The next week Perseus kept them so busy with movers, visits to the designer shops for clothes, a trip to the university to return her collage, appointments with the doctor to get their blood tests and have her stitches removed, that her graduation day came around before she knew it.

Since her mother's death, she'd thought her commencement would be a bittersweet experience because her parent wasn't there to see her graduate. What she hadn't counted on was Perseus being in the audience among all the proud parents and families to watch her receive her diploma.

She found it amazing that he would bother to come and support her. It deepened her feelings for him as nothing else could have done. Yet she didn't dare express them. All she could do was thank him for being there, for sharing in her happiness over a hard-fought personal battle in which she'd finally triumphed. His presence turned it into a major highlight she would always remember. *And treasure*.

On the night of her graduation, they stayed at the penthouse atop the Kostopoulos building. Sam went to bed in the guest room, so exhausted she was asleep by the time her head touched the pillow.

The next morning at ten, she found herself being chauffeured in Perseus's private limo to the church. He'd dressed for their wedding in a midnight blue suit and immaculate white shirt. She wore a knee-length white lace dress he'd picked out for her, a spray of gardenias on her shoulder and a shoulder-length lace mantilla.

When she questioned why they were having a religious rather than a civil ceremony, he explained it was the only way to avoid unwanted publicity. As a personal favor to Perseus, the priest would close the doors of the church to the public while he conducted the forty-five-minute ceremony.

Sam started to panic. "I—I won't know what to do."

"All you have to do is imitate me," he explained in his deep, vibrant voice. "We'll both wear a garland of orange blossoms linked by ribbons, and we'll carry a candle. When the time comes, we'll follow the priest around the altar and drink wine from the common cup. At that point you will be *Kyria Kostopoulos*."

It seemed like a sacrilege to take part in such a beautiful and sacred ceremony when Sam knew their marriage was a sham. As they entered the old, beautiful Greek church, and their footsteps resounded in the quiet interior, Sam had the sudden urge to turn and run.

Perseus must have sensed her turmoil because she felt a firm hand clasp her elbow and escort her to the front where the priest and the two witnesses awaited them.

Dr. Strike greeted her warmly. The other gentleman,

Mr. Paulos, turned out to be one of Perseus's New York attorneys. Until Perseus told her that the other man was his legal right hand in the States, she hadn't realized how much she'd been living in a fantasy world for the last week.

When the time came, Mr. Paulos would probably be the one to handle their divorce. No. Not divorce. In all probability an annulment, since Perseus had made it perfectly clear they wouldn't be sleeping together.

That knowledge brought her down to earth with a vengeance, and robbed her of the joy she'd been feeling. *Foolish, foolish girl.*

The predominantly English ceremony began with occasional passages in Greek. There was an air of unreality as they began their walk behind the priest, symbolic of their walk through life. Each time they stopped, the sweet smoke of the incense he carried permeated the air she breathed.

Between that and the strong scent of the flowers, she started to feel faint, but an ever-watchful Perseus clasped her around her slender waist. He didn't let go when they stood before the priest to exchange vows.

"Do you, Samantha Telford, take Perseus Kostopoulos to be your wedded husband?"

"Yes." *With all my heart*, she murmured inwardly. No matter how bogus this wedding might be, she loved Perseus. *Her* part of the ceremony would not be a lie.

The pressure of his hand seemed to tighten a fraction before the priest asked in a solemn voice, "Do you, Perseus Kostopoulos, take Samantha Telford to be your wedded wife?"

"I do," came the fervent response. Perseus was such a wonderful actor, he sounded as if the vows actually meant something to him.

As much as she wanted to look at him, she didn't dare because her greatest fear was that she'd give herself away when he kissed her. To her shock, that moment never came, nor did she hear the priest say anything about pronouncing them man and wife. Instead, he extended her a cup of wine.

Her hands trembled as she lifted it to her lips and took a sip. Then it was Perseus's turn. She watched him drink from the same spot where her lips had been.

At that moment his gaze collided with hers. Maybe it was the shadowy light of the interior, but for a brief second his dark eyes seemed to hold a possessive, even primitive gleam that acted like a jolt of electricity to her sensitized body.

In the next instant he removed the flower garland from her lace-covered head. A strange smile hovered at the corner of his compelling mouth as he found her left hand and placed a ring with one exquisite teardrop-shaped diamond on her finger.

"Make no mistake, *Kyria*. We're married in the eyes of God and the world. I'm your husband now."

Until you no longer need me, her heart cried out in fresh anguish because she wanted this wedding to be real.

Robbed of even the traditional ceremonial kiss, she averted her eyes and began accepting the congratulations of their small audience. In a few minutes, Perseus was escorting her from the church, explaining that his private plane was waiting to take them to Wyoming. A celebratory lunch had been prepared on board.

The events of the next week passed by in a kind of blur. Not only did they take care of the headstone and her mother's burial, Perseus insisted on being at her side as she visited with distant relatives and a few old friends of her mother's. Then they were winging their way to Greece.

Sam had never been out of the U.S. before. Her husband of two weeks, seated across from her on the plane, could have no comprehension of the tumultuous emotions warring within her since his entry into her life.

Everything was happening to her for the first time, increasing her ecstasy as well as her trepidation: marriage, her ride in his company jet, the stringent taste of retsina, the promised view of the ancient Acropolis she'd only glimpsed from history books, or through films.

Since she didn't own a TV set or a VCR, she hadn't watched that many videos. In ways, she felt like a child who'd just been born, marveling at every precious new moment of life unfurling.

Perhaps because of the pace Perseus had set, combined with the emotional upheaval he'd brought into her life, Sam was too exhausted to do anything more than go straight to his apartment and bed when they reached Athens.

She half heard him say something to the effect that now they'd returned to his native land, she was to begin playing her part as his bride by day.

Since she'd thought that was what she'd been doing all along, she didn't understand what he meant. The problem was, she was too dead on her feet to ask for clarification. Before closing her bedroom door, she assured him she would follow through on their contract. He would have nothing to complain about.

He murmured something she didn't understand before he told her to go bed. She gladly obeyed him, and fell into a dreamless sleep, knowing nothing for the next fifteen hours.

CHAPTER FOUR

SAM loved it all—the heat, the overcrowding, the smells, the traffic jams, the cacophony of sounds produced by loquacious city dwellers huddled together in charming, shady cafés at various neighborhood squares.

As she darted a farewell glance to Athens through the smoked glass of the Kostopoulos limousine, she heard her husband say, "Forget Archbishop Kominatos's assertion that one cannot look upon Athens without tears. Instead, recall the words of Pericles who told us to remember the greatness of Athens as she really is, and fall in love with her."

"I see no faults," Sam protested, loving every new experience since they'd left his downtown apartment.

"Then you're one of those rare tourists blessed to ignore her defects," came the wry rejoinder. "We can still take the helicopter to Serifos. All you have to do is say the word and I'll instruct the chauffeur to drive us to my office where there's a helipad."

Her head whipped around, and she put out a placating hand. It didn't quite touch his arm with its golden brown skin she could see through the dark hairs. "Oh, no, Perseus. Please— I'm longing to take the ferry."

"It's a five hour ride in ninety-five degree heat."

"But I *love* the water. I've only ever been on the ferries in Hudson Bay which isn't the same thing as you well know. This is *Greece*!" she cried with all the enthusiasm of her soul.

His deep chuckle found its way to her insides. He must think her an absolute idiot, but she didn't care. She was quite certain this was one great big dream, that one day she'd wake up in her tiny New York apartment frantically looking for a real job to afford the necessities of life now that she was a college graduate.

Everyone knew that once you had your degree, it took at least two to five years to find a decent job. Even then, you might never work in your chosen field of endeavor.

But if this dream didn't vanish right away, she was going to be able to market her best designs and create new ones, thanks to the enigmatic man seated next to her reading the daily newspaper in a language she was determined to learn as quickly as possible.

"What are you concentrating on so hard?" he queried unexpectedly.

Sam thought he'd forgotten she was there. "I'm working on my Greek. According to one of the brochures your maid brought with my breakfast, we're going to the *limani* to take a *vapori*."

He threw his head back and actually laughed. The sound thrilled her. "Excellent, Kyria Kostopoulos."

Mrs. Kostopoulos. She loved her new title. Her secret prayer was that she'd never have to relinquish it.

"I'm pleased you took the time to look through them. Now say the words after me, and you will be able to make yourself understood to any of my countrymen."

Throughout the short seven-mile drive to one of the three harbors of Piraeus, she was given her first lesson in Greek by a master.

By the time they'd arrived at the port, she was able to say *kalimera* which meant good morning, *chero poli*, which meant how do you do, and *ya sas*, which meant goodbye. All of which she tried out on their chauffeur who grinned from ear to ear, then complimented her before whispering something in rapid Greek to Perseus whose broad smile made him appear years younger and much more attractive than ever.

She didn't like to think about him being younger because that brought up the past, the reason why she was here posing as his temporary wife. In reality, he would go to his grave loving the fiancée who'd once spurned him, and now wanted him back.

Well, she wasn't going to get him back. Sam was here to see to that. Already she felt territorial and protective of her bridegroom, and if that woman dared try anything...

A warm, solid arm unexpectedly slid around her shoulders and he hugged her to his chest.

Sam's heart started to hammer.

What was Perseus doing? The pleasure was too great.

"Such fierce thoughts on this beautiful summer morning," he whispered against her neck, sending a tingling sensation of delight through her body. "What could have turned your eyes the color of smoke?" The soft pressure of his lips on her tender skin was almost her undoing.

Steady, Sam. He warned you that he expected you to act like his enamored bride while he played the role of the loving husband in public. Never forget that pertinent fact for a second.

He's not taking you to the island via the ferry for your sake. He's using this opportunity to create gossip which will precede him to Serifos. To the woman he still loved...

Before Sam had ever met Perseus, she knew he was hounded by the news media, but she had no idea how bad it was until now. Every step they took, some reporter was lurking nearby to take a picture and exploit him any way they could.

For once however, it seemed he wanted it known that he was returning to his native village with a new bride in tow. And all for the sake of the fiancée who was awaiting him with open arms, prepared to grovel for his forgiveness.

Over my dead body...

"To be honest, Perseus, I'm overwhelmed by so much attention," she answered back, clutching the lapel of his cream-colored sport shirt to steady herself while they were stopped partway up the gangway of the crowded ferry.

Despite the chaos surrounding them, the clean tang of the soap he'd used in the shower filled her senses. The heat tended to bring out its subtle, lemony fragrance. His masculine appeal drowned out her awareness of anything else. Because he was wearing sunglasses, she couldn't see into his eyes. Maybe it was just as well since she'd started making a habit of it.

He smoothed a thumb over the curve of her cheek. "You'll learn to forget that everyone's watching. Just concentrate on me, and follow my lead. When we reach Serifos, we'll be left alone."

Except that *she'll* be there, Sam lamented inwardly.

With his hand against her back, he urged her forward and they took their place on deck among the crowd.

He'd had their luggage sent on ahead. Except for her tote bag, they carried nothing with them. She clasped the rail, enjoying the gentle breeze as the ferry worked its way out of the harbor. The day would prove to be a scorcher, but right now the temperature was bearable and the fantastic view of the boats and water beyond her power to describe.

Perseus stood behind her with his arms wrapped around her slender waist, his chin buried in her hair. Today a white ribbon contained her gleaming gold mane.

She'd never worn white before and had been surprised at the shop that the modest sundress and sleeveless jacket with its colorful embroidery on the bodice and hem looked good on her. A perfect fit down to the underwear, hose and leather sandals, he'd purchased an entire wardrobe for her. Except for a few items, everything would be waiting for her on Serifos.

To anyone looking, they were typical honeymooners whispering to each other, staying as physically close together as decency permitted. That was the stipulation he'd laid down before they'd taken vows at the church. Whenever there was an audience, she was to become the besotted bride and hold nothing back.

To her shock, the role of playing wife came naturally to her. Too naturally. She was enjoying every moment of their time together. His strong heartbeat against her back dictated the pounding of her own.

Within the confines of his arms she experienced a sense of rightness and security she'd be loathe to give up when their marriage ended. How could that be when she'd only known him a few weeks?

"Perseus?"

"Hmm..." He sounded as bemused as she felt.

"Tell me a little bit about your fiancée so I'll know what to expect. Forewarned is forearmed," she said, trying to sound casual. They'd talked about many things, but he had yet to satisfy her curiosity where his past was concerned.

"I haven't seen her in twenty years. The girl who stabbed me before disappearing will have come back a woman."

"You're evading my question," Sam bit out frustratedly. "*Why* did she stab you?"

After an ominous pause, "When we said our vows to each other on Delos, she must have thought we were playing some kind of game. I was the dangerous, forbidden fruit from the lowest class of society, the kind of boy you didn't marry, but had fun stringing along.

"When I appeared in her bedroom, intent on taking her away with me so we could be married, she got her first clue that I was serious. Frightened and repulsed by the depth of my feelings for her, she panicked and did what came naturally to protect herself."

Sam shook her head. "But you would never have forced her. I *know* you wouldn't have, so what she did to you wasn't the least bit natural!"

"But it was human," he murmured against her temple where her pulse throbbed madly. "The women from my country have fiery temperaments, and she was young, only eighteen."

"Nothing excuses criminal behavior, Perseus. I don't know how you can excuse her." Sam's voice shook. "But I guess it's true that real love can overcome any obstacle, even cruelty."

"Love *is* cruel, and sometimes wonderful, Kyria Kostopoulos. One day even *you* will fall victim to it, experiencing glorious heights and agonizing depths. At that point your understanding will surpass guesswork."

Because of an unwise love, her own mother had suffered tremendous pain. Sam started to tremble. "I don't think I want to know."

He clasped her tighter. "That's the problem. Love doesn't ask if it can come to stay. When we least expect it, it arrives full-blown, and we're never the same again."

Thankfully he couldn't see the tears welling in her eyes. "*You've* never been the same."

"No," came the haunting reply.

Her heart went out to him. "I—I want to help you, Perseus." Her voice caught.

"Then stay close to me. Don't let me out of your sight. Above all, always be yourself, no matter the circumstances. Be the woman who in her righteous indignation called me Mr. Kofolopogos, and told me she wasn't intimidated by my bellowing."

Sam lowered her head, embarrassed. "I can't believe I said those things to you."

"I shall never forget them," he murmured against the nape of her neck. His fleeting kiss turned her bones to liquid. It was a good thing she was holding on to the railing or she would have fallen.

"Come. Let's go below. This air makes me thirsty for a cup of my own kind of coffee. If memory serves me, we'll enjoy *negraki* with it."

"Is that some kind of pastry?"

"It's chocolate cake made with rum and raisins, topped with devilishly rich chocolate sauce."

She smiled up at him. "That's right. You love sweets."

"How do you know that?"

"Because you eat dessert with every meal, and the tea you made me caused the spoon to stand on end."

His bark of laughter prompted heads to turn in their direction. Ignoring their audience, they made their way to the lower deck, their arms around each other's waists.

Like lovers.

But they weren't lovers. They were conspirators attempting to pull off a desperate charade. What if she failed him?

After fulfilling her three wishes with a humbling generosity she didn't know any human possessed to that high a degree, the fear that she might let *him* down had become her worst nightmare. But thus far, he didn't seem to have reservations or complaints over her performance.

He found them a table at a window, then summoned the waiter. Though she'd had a roll and juice at the hotel before they'd left Athens, she found that she still had room for chocolate cake. The rum gave it a different, marvelous flavor. She could see why Perseus ordered a second helping with his coffee.

He reminded her of an eager, hungry little boy who instantly discarded what he didn't want in favor of the things he consumed with relish.

She wished she had pictures of him passing from

babyhood through the various stages of adolescence to his teenage years. What had he looked like—been like—when he'd first met the woman he'd made his fiancée, before that soul-destroying love had rebounded on him? Before making him retreat within himself, turning him into a wealthy, worldly-wise cynic who'd never been able to fall in love again?

Worried he'd key in to her personal thoughts, she decided to change the subject. "I can see an island in the distance."

"We're passing Kea. One day soon I'll take you there. The sea is crystal clear. You'll think you're bathing in sunlight."

"I want to explore every island!" she enthused.

For the moment he'd removed his sunglasses and his black gaze was studying her over the rim of his coffee cup. "Given a hundred years or so, you just might be able to accomplish that feat. While you're my wife, I'll do my best to take you to as many as time allows."

"That sounds wonderful. You know them all, don't you?"

"In the Cyclades, to be sure."

Taking a deep breath she ventured, "How did you get your start? I don't mean to be presumptuous, but if I'm supposed to—be married to—"

"There's no supposed about it," he interjected coolly. "You're my legal wife for as long as I need you. We struck a bargain and I've already fulfilled my part of it."

Sam froze. She hated it when that remote, dark side of him emerged seemingly out of nowhere. "I know that, Perseus. Every time I express a desire for anything, it's granted, just like magic. Y-you've already spoiled me beyond recognition. But I only meant that if our marriage were for real, a-and—"

"And we were sleeping together—" came the mocking insinuation.

She crushed the napkin in her fist. "I *meant*—" Her eyes flashed. "If we had met under other circumstances, and in the natural course of events had fallen in love and married, then I would know the most important things about you."

"You already know about Sofia." His voice grated.

Sofia.

Sam wondered when he'd finally reveal his fiancée's name. Already she hated it, hated what the other woman had done to him.

"I realize that, Perseus. But I need to know more about your beginnings, your own family. Do you have family on the island?"

The deafening silence between them made her wish she'd never asked the question, but it wasn't in her nature to keep still. She imagined he was already regretting his impulsive decision to marry her. A desperate man on a desperate mission, no doubt he was beginning to realize he'd made a ghastly mistake.

"I don't remember my father," he suddenly began in a low, pitchless voice. "He was a fisherman who died at sea before I turned a year old."

So far, Sam could relate to his story. As far as she was concerned, her own father had always been dead to her, too.

"For years it was just my mother and me. Mother wasn't that well. As soon as I could, I worked all the hours God gave me to eke out an existence for the two of us. When I had enough money saved, I made her visit the local doctor who was a widower with a child.

"It turned out my mother was severely anemic. Even so, she was a beautiful woman. Men had always come around her, but she never responded to any of them. The doctor began treatments, but after the initial visit, he didn't charge for them. That's when I realized that like the other men on the island, he'd become enamored of her.

"I suppose I was a typical little boy who loved my mother and didn't see any reason for a third party to disrupt our lives. I grew to dislike him very much. He didn't like me either. When mother wasn't present, he treated me like the dirt under his feet."

Sam could imagine how hard that would have been on a proud son who'd done everything to keep them alive. She felt a pain pierce her heart.

"On the other hand, I had to admit I'd never seen her looking or feeling better. It was selfish of me not to want her to get married. One day I heard them fighting over me. She told him she couldn't be his wife unless he accepted me as his son.

"He said he had a well-to-do brother in Athens who needed someone to help him in his shop. I could go and live with him and his wife."

At that revelation, Sam had to swallow the sickness welling up in her throat.

"Mother refused to listen and told him it was over between them. They stopped seeing each other for a few weeks. Then one day, as I was entering the house where we rented a room, I could hear voices. Apparently he'd made up with her and said I could come and live with them.

"Mother approached me about it. If I hadn't seen how miserable she was when she thought he'd gone out of her life permanently, I wouldn't have told her I was happy for her.

"So, they were married. At the age of thirteen, I went with my mother to live in his house which seemed like a palace to me. In front of mother, he showed me a modicum of deference. When she wasn't present, he couldn't tolerate me and relegated me to a smaller room at the back, away from the view of the sea.

"I didn't mind. It was more luxurious than the hovel we'd come from on the other side of the island. He and I never exchanged words, but there was a tacit agreement between us that I would not interfere in the marriage, that I would be seen but not heard, that I would not consider myself a part of the household except when protocol demanded. Most of all, I would not associate with his daughter, Sofia, who was my age, and attended private school."

Sofia was his sister through marriage? Sam moaned, hardly able to take it in. Her eyes closed tightly. Five years under one roof was more than enough time for adolescent love to flower into adult love, the painful kind—the kind you never got over...

"To his everlasting horror, Sofia had a mind of her own. I was off-limits, but it seemed I was the one novelty she couldn't resist. Needless to say, I fell hopelessly in love with her," he added with a depth of emotion Sam wished she hadn't heard.

"Since I knew her father considered me the lowest dregs of society, I made the decision to become the one man he'd eventually be forced to look up to."

Those words could have been taken right out of the age-old Greek myth, Sam mused with an aching heart.

"What? No wedding present?" yelled King Polydectes.

"I don't have any money," exclaimed Perseus.

"That's what you get for a lazy, good-for-nothing," said Polydectes.

Perseus was furious. "I can bring you any present in the world. Anything!" he said.

"Then bring me the head of Medusa."

"Fine!" Perseus shouted.

And like the Perseus of old, this modern-day Greek

hero, rejected by his love and scorned by her father, had gone off on a perilous voyage. After twenty years, he was returning home triumphant, with a temporary bride to defeat his enemies.

No one in the world but Sam knew how much Perseus was counting on her to carry off her part. Only now had she been given a glimpse of the frightening task ahead of her. She couldn't stop shaking, and needed answers to many more questions.

Her eyes searched the bleakness of his. "Will your mother be there to greet you?"

"No," came the quiet aside. "A year after I left Serifos, my mother asked for a divorce and came to live with me in Athens. Twelve months later, she died in my arms of pneumonia."

He must have seen the sheen of tears in Sam's eyes because he murmured, "Don't be sad. We didn't have one unhappy day."

"But you were so young to lose her. Was her husband cruel to her? Is that why she left him?"

"No. He was very good to her, but she couldn't forgive his treatment of me, or Sofia's actions."

"I love your mother already!" Sam blurted.

A sudden smile transformed his features. "You would have come as a delightful surprise to her, too. Because her health was always fragile, I've never regretted her death till this moment."

Beneath the compliment, Sam stirred uncomfortably. "I think I'm thankful that she's not alive to learn that her son didn't end up with the woman of his dreams after all."

Like the brilliant sun suddenly disappearing behind a thunderhead, his smile vanished. "There are worse fates, Kyria Kostopoulos."

Naturally after the stabbing, Perseus's mother would

have been like a mother lion with her adored cub, guarding him with her life, wanting only joy for him.

In that respect, Sam was grateful his mother hadn't lived to see this day— Perseus arriving home with a counterfeit bride.

She pushed her seat back and stood up. "If you'll excuse me, I need to use the powder room."

"Of course, but don't take too long. We're passing Kythnos. You'll enjoy the sight of the windmills. That particular island has great significance for me."

Her heart pounded far too hard to be healthy. "Why is that?" She had a feeling he was going to share another intimate memory about him and Sofia. Sam didn't want to hear it.

"You asked about my beginnings. As my bride, you're entitled to an explanation.

"It was there, at the thermal springs, whose radioactive waters are considered to be beneficial to many maladies, that I received the inspiration to market the water in locally made glass bottles, and sell them to the tourists at Piraeus.

"Such a simple concept. With one trip, I made enough money to buy a fishing boat. At that point I sold not only bottled thermal water, but fish. I had so much success, many vendors at the harbor paid me handsomely to supply them. In time, I was able to buy one vendor out, then another.

"Soon I bought a fleet of boats, some for fishing, others for pleasure. I discovered that wealthy tourists would pay me ten times my asking price when I took them to an uncharted island with virgin beaches for the day, and made certain they caught fish.

"Word traveled that I was the man to package the best tours in the Cyclades. I rented an office in Athens and set up my travel business. By this time I had contacts supplying me hand-painted icons and ceramics from

Mykonos, local pottery from Sifnos, embroidered goods and crafts from Naxos.

"As time went on, I hunted for properties and buildings which were being foreclosed on. With a minimum of refurbishing, I could resell them for a great deal more money than the original purchase price. Through investments, I was led to more ambitious endeavors, such as the purchase of larger ships, freighters to export goods."

Sam's eyes rounded in awe at each revelation falling from his lips. He made it sound so easy, when in fact she knew that only one man in several billion was even born with his kind of know-how and genius. Even then, the driving force behind such colossal success lay in the need to blot out the pain brought on by one woman. *Sofia.*

The more Perseus admitted Sam into his confidence, the more frightened she became of this faceless woman who would know with a woman's instincts that his marriage to an American college student fourteen years younger than himself was a total sham.

"*Now* no one knows as much about me as you do," he said, sounding curiously pleased with himself.

"Thank you for telling me," she mumbled. "I—I'll hurry."

"I'll be waiting. Then it will be your turn to tell me why you're so afraid of men. Me, in particular..."

That was one subject she would never discuss with Perseus, she vowed as she went to the ladies' room, then joined her husband on deck when it was time to disembark.

"*Look this way, Mrs. Kostopoulos.*"

Caught off guard by the man speaking American English in the midst of foreign conversation exploding all around them, Sam turned her head and met the flash of a camera.

Muttering a torrent of Greek which didn't need translation, Perseus tightened his arm around her waist. He ushered her through the crowds to a car waiting for them close to the pier.

Once they were ensconced in the back, and he'd introduced her to Yanni, the driver, he said, "Welcome to Serifos, your new home, Kyria Kostopoulos. Another day we will explore Livadi to your heart's content. Right now a cold shower and iced drinks are in order."

He was right. The sun's rays were pitiless. After Perseus's suggestion, Sam could think of nothing more divine. Yet the charming horseshoe-shaped beach below the adorable little cube-shaped white houses and churches made her long to investigate every square inch.

The bare, undulating hills of this island dotted with fertile valleys and a fairy-tale Venetian castle, had been Perseus's playground from birth, and as such was very precious to her.

Sam craned her head to see everything. "Do you live way up high in that village?"

He chuckled. "No. Panagia may offer a spectacular view, but I prefer to be on the water. A few years ago, I purchased beachfront property where I once fished and bodysurfed. I hired an architect to design a small villa in the Cycladic style, then had it built and furnished. It's around the other side of the island, totally private."

This has to be a dream. When are you going to wake up, Sam?

"How long have you lived here?"

"I haven't. For the last twenty I've worked out of Athens. However, from time to time I've flown here by helicopter to confer with the builder and oversee the construction.

"Serifos is my home," he stated in a voice of unashamed longing. "My roots run deep on this island. I've yearned to return and make it my future. Now everything is done except the landscaping. I've decided I'm putting you in charge of that project."

She shook her head in dazed consternation. "What do you mean?"

"Exactly what I said," he murmured with a trace of a smile turning up the corners of his mouth.

"I couldn't. I couldn't possibly," she cried out, aghast. "I—I don't know the first thing about being a gardener!"

"You know about color, composition, texture. I've witnessed your glorious sense of design with my own eyes."

Glorious? Did he have any idea that when he said things like that, joy filled her being until she felt giddy?

"The only difference is that you'll be working with growing things."

"But Perseus, I—"

"You promised to act the part of my bride," he broke in smoothly. "We'll have times when we work apart. But it's important to me that when we are together, we share more interests than a swim in the pool or a romp in the sea. Putting in a yard will make you feel our home is as much yours as mine."

"I—I don't think—"

"Shh…" he warned, putting his arm around her to draw her to his side, "or Yanni will assume we're having a lover's quarrel. Since he's one of the biggest gossips on the island, this ought to channel the course of his thoughts."

Quite how he managed it, Sam didn't know, but she suddenly found herself in his lap, his mouth descending on hers.

His lips brushed hers softly, as if testing their willingness to be kissed. "Your mouth hints of wild honeysuckle whose petals unfurl with the heat. Such delight I haven't tasted in a very long time. Pretend I'm the sun and open them to me.''

His voice sounded deep and husky. How did he imitate the kind of emotion that said he was dying for her kiss, when she knew this performance was for Yanni's benefit? Yanni, whose tongue would carry tales far enough to reach Sofia's ears.

This was wrong. But for the life of her, Sam had never known any sensation as pleasurable as the feel and taste of his mouth coaxing her lips apart to feast on the sweetness within.

As the pressure of his mouth increased, little shivers of ecstasy rippled through her body. He brought her right up against his chest, engulfing her in heart-throbbing sensuality.

She'd been kissed before, but she'd always been too aware of what she was doing, the mechanics. This was so different. With Perseus, there wasn't only an exquisite bonding of lips, mouths, bodies. She felt her soul leap to merge with his. The totality of their embrace made her forget the ordinary conventions of time and place.

This new level of communion with Perseus was more desirable than anything she'd ever experienced before. Then the frightening thought occurred that this could easily become the *only* form of communication which would satisfy her from here on out.

CHAPTER FIVE

"I-I'M Q-QUITE sure we've convinced Yanni by now," she stammered a few minutes later, hiding her flushed face in his neck. She was struggling for breath because he'd untied the ribbon in her hair to test its silky weight with his fingers.

"To be absolutely certain, stay right where you are and don't move a centimeter until we reach the villa."

Whether a command or not, she couldn't have done anything else but obey. He held her sensitized body cradled in his arms while his hands memorized the shape of her head, the length of her hair splayed over his hard-muscled arm.

"Only the gods could come up with a formula to create anything as miraculous as one golden strand of this gossamer mane." The sound of wonder in his voice was only increased by her own sense of awe that he would say these incredible things to her.

She was on the verge of forgetting this was an act on his part, and lifted her head to tell him this couldn't go on. In the process, her lips accidentally brushed against his scar. She quite forgot what she was going to say and blurted, "Does it ever hurt you, Perseus?"

"No. But if it repulses you, or makes you pity me, I'll go in for plastic surgery."

In her anger she cried, "Repulses me? How could you even say such a thing! Don't you know it makes you more interesting than you already are?"

Once again she'd spoken her true feelings without thinking, but it was too late now.

"As for feeling sorry for you, you couldn't be further

from the truth. To be honest, the thought came to me that if I were a man, I know I wouldn't want to tangle with you. I'd probably be thinking that if you had a scar, then the other poor devil must have come off much worse."

She heard the rich sound of laughter deep in his throat. "The possibility of you being a man is too inconceivable to warrant this discussion. Still, I'm thinking of having a plastic surgeon take a look."

"That is entirely your decision."

"Wrong. From here on out, I plan to consult you on everything, and expect you to do the same with me, otherwise our marriage will be less than it could or should be."

Though he didn't know it, Perseus had just put his finger on what she secretly believed ought to constitute a good marriage. But such a presumption was based on the premise that the two people involved were madly in love with each other. Hardly the case with her and—

"*Parakalo, Kyrie Kostopoulos*—"

Sam was thankful the driver had spoken up. She used the small interruption to slide off of Perseus. He seemed reluctant to let her go. Only then did she realize the car had stopped in front of the newly constructed villa.

She felt a slow wave of heat invade her body. Who knew how long Yanni had been waiting to alert them that they'd reached their destination?

How clever of Perseus to sidetrack her until she appeared to be the smitten bride who probably would have stayed in his arms another hour and still never noticed anything going on around them.

Like taking candy from a baby, he'd manipulated the situation to his advantage. No doubt he handled all his business decisions with the same flawless technique and finesse. Why should that surprise or shock her?

When she thought about it, their marriage was simply

another one of his business arrangements, albeit one with
a great deal more at stake than money alone.

Of course, no one had forced her into doing anything.
She'd entered into the contract of her own free will because she wanted to be near Perseus at any cost, so she
had absolutely no room to complain at his methods. If
on the ferry she'd felt an overwhelming compassion for
Perseus, and had told him she wanted to help any way
she could, then that was her problem, not his.

As he pointed out earlier, he'd paid for her coopera-
tion in advance.

Now she owed him. When they'd struck their bargain,
she had no way of knowing she'd be transported by his
lovemaking. Until today he hadn't revealed the sensuous
side of his nature. It never occurred to her that she was
capable of such a passionate physical response.

Hadn't her mother admitted to the same thing happening to her when she'd met Sam's father? A magical
bonding which had swept her away, nullifying any pre-
conceived ideas of a gentle, sensible love which would
allow her to stay in control and not lose her identity?

But a passion like that could never last. When it had
burned itself out, her father—who suffered no remorse
because he had no conscience—had gone off to pursue
his selfish life, leaving her mother pregnant and alone.

In the last half hour Sam had been given a little taste
of what ecstasy was all about, and she wanted no part
of it. Fortunately her situation and that of her mother's,
bore little resemblance. There would be no morning after
for Sam.

No way. She was Perseus's *daytime* bride only.

Oh, yes, she'd play house with him until he was strong
enough to withstand Sofia's wiles. But Sam would throw
all her energies into the thriving new business she was
going to create for herself. On the day he set her free,

she'd leave Greece a successful artist in her own right, able to maintain a career and flaunt it in her father's face.

With the image of his faithlessness continually before her, Sam would never allow a man to do to her what her father had done to her mother.

Perhaps in that regard, Sam and Perseus had one thing in common. Rejection in any form tended to put life into perspective and focus a human being on a particular path. In Perseus's case, he'd carved an empire out of nothing.

In her own way, Sam was determined to do the same thing. The bargain they'd struck could only speed up the process.

With Perseus's help, she alighted from the car, then gasped. The stunning chalk-white villa set against a backdrop of impossibly blue sea and sky made her feel as if she'd been transported to another world.

Yet because of Perseus's suggestion, already in her mind's eye she could imagine the stark serenity broken up by evergreens, sweet-smelling honeysuckle and uneven flower clusters of brilliant orange, deep shocking fuchsia pink, vermilion and lemon yellow, set right up against the walls of the villa.

A garden gone wild, yet painstakingly tended to make it appear so, as if color from nature's pallet had accidentally spilled in clumps, creating a unique and breathtaking masterpiece.

Her eyes narrowed as her gaze ran from the front of the house to the sea. She could envision a geometric garden in keeping with the Geometric age of eighth-century Greece. An exquisite melange of oleander blue, periwinkle, lavender and darkest plum, all in perfect order like a complicated mosaic.

The ideas were coming fast and furiously, causing the hairs on the back of her neck to stand on end. She could hardly wait to get to her sketchpad.

Never in her wildest dreams had she considered creating a real, live landscape. Now, for some unknown reason, she couldn't imagine anything more wonderful than crafting a design made of growing things. Her fingers fairly itched to dig into rich topsoil and plant her newly conceived garden with loving care...

Without conscious thought she said, "Perseus? H-how soon do you want me start on the yard?"

He was standing behind her, his hands on her shoulders in a gentle yet possessive grip. She swayed as he brushed the side of her cheek with his lips, caught off guard by the sensuous gesture.

"It appears my idea has appealed so much, it has already taken root. You're miles away from me." But there was a wealth of satisfaction in his words.

You're wrong, Perseus. Since the first moment we met, you danced straight into my heart, changing the life-giving rhythm of that vital organ for all time.

"But to answer your question, tomorrow you can begin in earnest. This afternoon we'll lunch, then nap. By this evening, we'll be ready for a swim in the sea. It's an experience unlike any other."

Suddenly she grew dizzy as he put an arm behind her knees and swept her up in his arms. "Welcome to the *Villa Danae*, Kyria Kostopoulos. Your home from now on," he murmured, then lowered his mouth to hers, blotting out the sun, stifling her little moan of protest that said this was only temporary.

Yanni had gone ahead of them and had opened the door of the villa so Perseus could carry her over the threshold in true marital tradition. Once again she could feel herself succumbing to the desire her new husband was encouraging her to share for his retainer's benefit.

Struggling for breath she finally said, "Danae is the name of Perseus's mother."

He raised his head so his black piercing eyes could

stare down at her. "That's right. You're familiar with the myth of the island?" He actually sounded pleased.

"Yes." *I know it by heart.*

"Tomorrow I'll take you to see the curious rock formations which resemble Medusa, Perseus and Danae."

Her senses leaped at the thought of spending the day with him, exploring new sites.

"You've named your home in honor of your own mother, haven't you?"

She heard him suck in his breath. "As it happens you are correct."

They had come out of the scorching sun into a blessedly cool foyer. He lowered her to the tile floor, no doubt a local island design done in multicolors against a white background which she found exquisite.

With his arm around her shoulders, he ushered her through an alcove to a spacious, uncluttered living room of white walls, handmade furniture and a few art treasures, which gave out on a stunning view of the sea.

"A very astute observation. I promised my mother that one day I'd return to Serifos and build her the kind of home she deserved. Unfortunately she died before I could prove my words."

The deep ache in Sam's heart over his pain intensified. A need to comfort him prompted her to say, "I have no doubts that she's been watching your progress with motherly pride. Something tells me she's smiling down on you right now."

His dark brows met in a frown. "You believe in a hereafter?"

"Of course. Nothing as marvelous as this world could just come to an end, with nothing else to look forward to!"

"Keep talking like that and you'll make me a believer."

"When my time comes, I fully expect to see my mother and be with her."

"And your father?" he interjected so smoothly, she would have had a hard time proving that he'd never thought to ask the question before.

Unfortunately, at the mention of her other parent, the magic vanished and Sam eased herself away from his arm. In panic, she wandered over to one of the nubby white couches upholstered in a kind of crewel work of the same hue. "I'd rather not talk about him if you don't mind."

"You always avoid the mention of him, but no matter. One day when I've won your complete trust, you'll tell me. In the meantime, meet Ariadne, my housekeeper."

Sam swung around in surprise, still pondering his remark about trust, and totally unaware that anyone else had come into the room.

"She's Yanni's wife. Together they take care of the villa."

"Welcome to Serifos, Kyria Kostopoulos." The fortyish-looking dark-haired woman with a thin, wiry build like her husband welcomed her in excellent English.

"Thank you, Ariadne. I didn't expect you to speak my language so beautifully. I'm hoping you'll teach me some Greek."

She looked to Perseus for permission before he gave her a nod of assent. "It would be a pleasure."

"*Efcharisto.*" Sam tried out the word the way Perseus had taught her to say it.

The older woman beamed. "Your lunch is ready whenever you say."

"What is the word for lunch?"

"*Messimergiano.*"

Sam tried to say it exactly the same way, producing a nod of approval from both her husband and his housekeeper.

"Give us five minutes, Ariadne. My wife needs to freshen up first. I'll show her to our suite."

"*Our* suite?"

"Relax," he murmured as he escorted her out of the room and through the foyer to the other side of the villa where the master bedroom faced the sea.

"Before you accuse me of breaking our contract, let me assure you that the room I plan to occupy adjoins this one through that connecting door. It has a lock you can turn against me every night."

The way he said the last made her feel like a silly, virginal, naive little schoolgirl who was terrified of her own shadow.

"A-actually," she stammered, "I do trust you completely and don't plan to use the lock."

His face became an inscrutable mask. "Perhaps you'd better. It wouldn't be wise to tempt the gods, not on *this* island," he warned in a haunting tone before turning away. "The bathroom is on your right," he called over his shoulder. "I'll be back in a few minutes to fetch you."

The modern air-conditioning worked so well, she felt a little chilly. Under the circumstances she decided not to discard the jacket of her sundress.

His warning kept reverberating in her head. She had no fears of his entering her bedroom uninvited. The horrible truth of the matter was, she feared that if she spent very much time here, it was *his* door that would need locking. *Against her.*

Terrified at the implications, she headed for the bathroom to freshen up, scarcely able to appreciate the simple, yet perfect decor of the large room with its king-size bed and dark wood furniture.

The furnishings exactly matched the aqua water and white sand she could see through the floor-to-ceiling glass doors facing his private stretch of beach. Further out, the sea they'd just crossed from Piraeus to Serifos reflected a vivid cobalt-blue color. That same tone had been picked up in the ethnic-styled lamp vases and floor tiles.

If she squinted, she couldn't tell where sea and sky stopped, and the room began. In her artist's opinion, there was no greater decorator on earth than nature. Perseus had created heaven in this ancient, serene oasis of the world. Only seventy-two miles from Athens, yet she felt they'd come to a forgotten region of the planet, away from the noise and chaos of civilization.

How tragic his mother wasn't alive to see what great things her son had accomplished. But even more tragic was his love for Sofia, a woman who'd brought him no joy, no children. Yet his soul still loved her, his proud jawline still carried the mark of her betrayal for all the world to see.

Sofia.

She was the only reason Sam was here on Serifos.

"You'd be wise to remember that salient fact," Sam said out loud to the image in the bathroom mirror.

To further awaken herself to the dangers of impossible dreams about Perseus, she sluiced her face with cold water, then reached for the fluffy, rose-colored towels. They matched the marble sink with its gold accessories.

Everything pleased her senses and invited, especially the fresh flowers, a combination of daisies and roses placed there for her enjoyment. Such luxury made Sam feel like she was moving about in some kind of fantastic dream not even her mind could have conjured.

Like a good fairy, it seemed Ariadne had been busy because all Sam's toiletries had been placed in the bathroom, her new clothes, shoes, everything put away in the cupboards and drawers of her bedroom.

After looking in the cabinet, she applied a little lemon splash cologne to her throat and wrists, then brushed her hair. It was while she was retying her gold mane with the white ribbon that she heard the telephone ring. It's piercing sound amid the stillness set off alarm bells in her head.

She supposed it could be a business call for Perseus, but she had the gut feeling the person on the other end of the line was none other than Sofia. No doubt word had reached her that Perseus and his new bride had arrived on the island and would have settled in his villa by now.

Because of Sam's collage, Perseus had never returned the phone call Sofia had made to his office in New York. Now that he'd arrived on Serifos, he was a sitting target.

Sam put down the hairbrush, her fear for Perseus making her heart pound too hard. She could feel it in her throat and coughed to dislodge the throbbing sensation.

"Kyria Kostopoulos?"

"Yes, Ariadne?" Sam hurried out of the bathroom to face the housekeeper standing in the doorway leading to the hall.

"There's a phone call for Perseus Kostopoulos, but he went for a short walk before lunch. The woman said that since he wasn't here, she would talk to you."

Sam shook her head in consternation. "She didn't give her name?"

"No. She only said that it was urgent."

Was it Sofia?

At the thought of talking to her, Sam's mouth went dry. "I—I don't speak any Greek yet, Ariadne."

The older woman shrugged her shoulders. "Perhaps she speaks English?"

Sam's gaze darted to the phone at the side of the bed. When she'd asked Perseus how she could help, he'd said, "Stay close to me. Never let me out of your sight."

But he'd never told her what to do when he'd deliberately gone out of her sight.

Was it a coincidence that he'd decided to take a walk at the precise moment Sofia called? Or had he purposely left Sam to run interference for him because he knew instinctively that Sofia would call, and he wasn't ready to face his former fiancée yet?

Was this Sam's first major test?

With fear and trepidation, she approached the bedside table. Saying a little prayer that she wouldn't let him down, she picked up the receiver.

"Hello?" She found she had to clear her throat. "This is Mrs. Kostopoulos."

"Thank you for taking my call." The woman spoke in heavily accented English. "My name is Sofia Leonidas. Do you know who I am?"

Sam clutched the receiver in a death grip.

What was she supposed to say to this woman? What did Perseus expect her to say?

"Yes. I've heard my husband speak of his extended family. I understand his mother was once married to your father, that at one time you and Perseus were stepbrother and sister."

The ominous silence on the other end of the line indicated Sam had hit some kind of a nerve.

"What Perseus and I shared only comes once in a lifetime, if then..."

The woman's fierce avowal of love sent Sam's heart plummeting to her feet.

"I tried to reach him in New York, but he never returned my call. After what I did to him so long ago, I don't blame him for refusing to have anything to do with me." Her voice shook with such emotion, Sam couldn't see how it was feigned.

"But there were life-and-death reasons why I did what I did. Reasons he deserves to hear before anyone else. I've been waiting twenty empty years to tell him."

The woman talking on the other end of the line didn't

sound at all like the cold, cruel young woman who'd stabbed Perseus before running off where he could never find her. Sofia Leonidas sounded like a woman deeply in love. Someone tormented and desperate.

"Now that Perseus is back in Serifos, I must talk to him. You see, my father is dying and has asked for him to come. He has many things to say to Perseus. So do I..." Her voice trailed off because she was sobbing.

"Once again this is a matter of life and death. You are his new bride. For him to finally marry after all these years means you have influence over him.

"I'm begging you to use that influence to get him to come over to the house. Though he has built himself a villa, this was once his home. For a little while, Papa was a father to him. As for myself, I loved him and still do. In fact I'll go to my grave with his name on my lips."

Sam shivered at the depth of the other woman's declaration.

"Would you please convey that message to Perseus? I've left the phone number with your housekeeper."

Sam took a fortifying breath. "I'll tell him what you said, but I can't promise anything else."

"Bless you for that much. It's more than I deserve."

The line went dead.

Sam sank down onto the side of the bed, completely stunned by the woman's importuning, and worse, her tears.

Sofia was still in love with Perseus, and something told Sam that when Perseus heard his fiancée's explanation—whatever it was—they'd be reunited.

So deep was her devastation over the probable outcome of their meeting, she didn't realize Perseus had come into the bedroom. He was in white running shorts and a black T-shirt.

She swallowed hard at the sight of his virile, masculine frame.

"Whom have you been talking to? Your face has lost all its color."

"That was Sofia."

His muscles tautened in reaction. He looked fiercely angry. The hands at his sides formed into fists.

"Why didn't you let Ariadne take the message?" he bit out with scarcely bridled fury which was completely uncharacteristic for him.

"Your housekeeper was the one who came to find me. She said the woman on the phone asked for me."

"Sofia didn't waste any time," he muttered with a savagery she'd never heard before.

Sam got up from the bed. "Before you say anything, you need to know that her father is dying and has been asking for you."

His head reared back. "*Dying*?"

She nodded. "Sofia also said there was a reason why she did what she did to you twenty years ago. She said it was a matter of life and death then, and now she needs to explain everything. She was sobbing, Perseus. I believe her tears were real."

His black eyes glittered dangerously. "What else did she say? I might as well hear all of it."

Averting her eyes so she wouldn't see the joy leap into his, Sam murmured, "She said that what you two shared could never be repeated in a lifetime, that after twenty long empty years, she's still in love with you. She also said that though she knows you could never forgive her, she will go to her grave with your name on her lips."

A mask came down over his face so she couldn't tell what he was thinking.

"I think you should go to her right away."

His face looked like thunder. "I have business on

Naxos and should have flown there an hour ago, but I'll be back to take you for a swim after dinner.''

He disappeared too fast for her to tell him she was sorry she'd offended him by saying something out of turn.

The rest of the day was pure disaster, and she had trouble eating more than a few bites of food the cook had prepared. She was ready to retire early when Perseus suddenly arrived back at the villa, and insisted that she join him for a swim.

"Don't venture too far out," Perseus called to her a few minutes later from the beach where he was drying off. He'd hunkered down to watch her, his well-shaped head black and sleek in the moonlight. She trembled before such a powerful aura.

"I'll stay close to shore. I promise."

Sam was still pinching herself because nothing about this night seemed real. Not the warm water, or the enormous grapefruit moon, or the balmy, velvety air.

The heat radiating off the sand had sent her splashing into the sea. After a vigorous workout, she floated on her back so she could look up at the heavens and still keep an eye on Perseus. Beyond him, the lights of the charming white villa beckoned.

His anger over Sofia's call had long since dissipated. Thank heaven that anger hadn't been directed at her. In fact, he seemed to be in a vastly different frame of mind than he had that morning.

"Did you enjoy the dinner I asked Maria to prepare for you?"

"It was wonderful. What was it called?"

"*Boxa*, a combination of succulent lamb, greens and a lemon sauce cooked in a special ceramic pot. For dessert I asked her to serve you some of that sweet, creamy *Mizithra* cheese. My favorite."

"Everything was delicious and much too fattening.

I'm going to have to stay out here all night to work off the extra calories."

He chuckled deep in his throat.

She'd said that as a pretext to keep her distance from him. The image of his superbly muscled frame with its mat of black hair, the fluid grace of his walk, the bronzed skin covering his magnificent physique set her pulse racing.

Just looking at him heated her own body several degrees. She could almost hear her skin sizzle as she entered the water. She could see the headlines now.

"Young American wife of Greek Tycoon ignites like a firecracker in front of their villa in the Cyclades, sending spurts of steam 100 feet into the atmosphere."

Her fanciful thoughts translated to gentle laughter. To her shock, he suddenly appeared beside her, treading water while his dark gaze narrowed on her animated features.

"When you smile that way, you resemble the woman in a painting I have hanging on the wall of my bedroom. I noticed the likeness the moment you first entered my office. Her hair resembles spun gold, as well, but it's much longer and swirls about her body. She's chained to a rock."

"It must be Andromeda. The woman Perseus rescued from the sea monster and brought home to Serifos."

He gave an imperceptible nod of his dark head. "She's almost as beautiful as you are."

Sam slipped beneath the water to hide her blush and resurfaced a few feet away. But in one swift movement he'd reached her side again, a devilish half smile curving the corner of his mouth. Right then he seemed to shed ten years.

To Sam he was so heartbreakingly handsome, she wanted to reach out and touch him, every beautiful part. Physically, he was perfect to her.

"Who was the artist?" She had to say something to break the enchantment.

"Jules Gregory. He wasn't well known when he came to Serifos to paint. I bought it off him at least sixteen years ago when he was a struggling artist. Now his portraits are sought after by the many art collectors.

"Personally, I still think the painting I own is his masterpiece. Maybe because he painted it at a time when he was suffering over a love affair which had gone wrong."

Sam had to school her features to show no reaction, but inside she was undergoing a near convulsion.

A frown brought back the worry lines in his face. In a lightning move he clasped her upper arms in a firm grip. "What's wrong? Did you just feel a cramp?"

"Yes." She nodded, grateful for any reason to end their enforced intimacy. "I guess I swam too hard after that huge meal."

"Come."

He gathered her in his powerful arms and carried her from the water to the villa without so much as a strained breath. By the time he'd deposited her in the bathroom of her suite and had started her shower, she was literally writhing from the heated contact of their bodies separated by nothing more than their bathing suits.

Hers was a modestly cut blue bikini which he'd picked out for her in New York. Even so, it displayed more flesh than she liked to reveal.

"Thank you for everything, Perseus." Her voice wobbled because his eyes were playing over her face and figure. "I'll be fine now." She reached for a huge bath towel and covered herself.

"I'm not so sure," he said on a solemn note. "Why are there shadows when your face was lit up like the sun a few minutes ago?"

He had the uncanny knack of seeing beneath the surface. That was part of what made him such a genius in the corporate world.

"I think jet lag has caught up with me. A good night's sleep will produce wonders."

He still didn't seem satisfied. "If you don't feel well and need me in the night, just call out and I'll come."

The temptation to do just that was almost more than she could bear. "You need your sleep, too," she murmured, needing to get away from him before she betrayed the feelings bursting to escape and find expression in one pair of arms.

"I'm used to flying. You're not," came the swift reply. "I think we'll postpone an exploration of the island tomorrow and simply lounge around the indoor pool."

He seemed totally concerned for her welfare, yet she retained niggling doubts that he might not want to be seen around the island with Sam. Not if he'd been to visit Sofia, and things had changed for him in some way.

"Tomorrow I'll have some gardening catalogs flown over from Athens to assist you. We can spend the day talking about our yard, and we won't have to lift a finger. How does that sound?"

A pain entered her heart. *It sounded very domestic and wonderful. The kind of thing married couples in love tended to do.*

"To be honest, I'm excited to get started."

"Then it's settled. Good night, Samantha. No doubt you prefer the shortened version, but you're entirely too feminine to go by the name of Sam." Before she knew how it had happened, he'd brushed her lips with his own in a featherlight caress, then he disappeared from the bathroom.

Samantha.

It was the first time he'd ever said her name. With that attractive Greek accent, he made it sound beautiful. While she stood there tingling from his kiss, her mind reeled from the personal comments he'd been making all evening when there'd been no audience to play to.

But after she'd been standing beneath the shower spray for ten minutes, she reasoned that he was doing everything in his power to make her feel at ease with him. No doubt he was preparing her for those times when they had to appear in public together. Her job was play along with Perseus and convince family and friends who knew Sofia that they were a married couple madly in love.

By the time she'd slid between the silky sheets, her body was begging for sleep. The only problem was her mind which refused to turn off.

Tomorrow she'd take a peek in his bedroom and see the painting he'd purchased from her derelict father so many years ago. How strange to think one of his creations hung in this villa. Stranger still was the fact that Perseus had loved it so much, he'd bought it when he was a much younger man and had taken it home with him, rather than display it in his New York or Athens office.

As she started to drift off, her thoughts came full circle to settle on Sofia. Despite all Perseus's plans, Sam had no doubts he'd eventually be united with his only true love.

By the time oblivion finally took over, her pillow was sopping wet and she slept without it.

CHAPTER SIX

WHEN she eventually awakened, she could tell the sun was almost overhead. She'd slept twelve hours and now her stomach was making hungry sounds.

One look in the mirror and she let out a cry. Her eyes were so puffy, they looked like slits. If Perseus saw her like this, he'd know she'd been crying. Maybe he'd heard her muffled sobs through the connecting door last night. Whatever, she'd wear her sunglasses out to the pool on the pretext that the light hurt her eyes.

After sifting through her new clothes, she found an attractive pair of beige linen shorts and matching sleeveless top trimmed in white. She toned the outfit with brown sandals and caught her hair back, fastening it with a tortoiseshell clip.

An application of pink frost lipstick, a touch of her favorite lemon cologne, and she felt ready to face the man with whom she had a contract, nothing more.

In the habit of making her bed, she tidied the room, then slipped out the doors to head for the kitchen. A glass of juice and a roll of some kind sounded good. She'd be able to fix those things herself without disturbing Maria.

But she hadn't counted on being intercepted by Perseus who was just coming from his study. He looked breathtakingly masculine in a pair of denim cutoffs and nothing else.

"Kalimera, Samantha." Once more she could feel his eyes traveling over her in male admiration.

"Kalimera, Perseus."

Sam swallowed with difficulty and quickly looked away, for fear he'd catch her staring at him.

"Did you sleep well?"

"Too well. Any light still hurts my eyes."

"You're a natural blonde. The sun in this part of Greece takes some getting used to. Follow me to the pool and we'll enjoy brunch together."

His delivery was so smooth, she had no way of telling if he knew the true reason for the sunglasses or not.

"And I presume you've already put in the work of seven men," she quipped as they made their way to the side of the villa where the enclosed rectangular pool joined the patio through a series of glass doors.

"Only seven?" came the teasing rejoinder.

Sam chuckled before helping herself to a veritable feast of fresh fruit, honey glazed ham, melt-in-your-mouth pastry, omelets, and juice.

She took one of everything before sitting down at the poolside table with him. "If I stay here much longer, you're going to have to fire Maria and put me to work in the kitchen. We'll both lose weight in a big hurry."

Now it was Perseus's turn to laugh. A low-pitched, full bodied sound that said she'd truly amused him.

"Luckily I've already hired you to put in my yard."

After popping another huge grape in her mouth she said, "I can't wait to get at it." And she meant it.

He eyed her over the rim of his coffee cup. "You already know what you're going to do. I saw it in your eyes yesterday. Are you going to let me in on it now, or do I have to wait for the finished product?"

"This is your villa, and as suc—"

"*Our* villa," he corrected her, looking lazily indolent stretched out on the lounger.

She wished he'd stop saying things like that. "Yes, well, I'd like to talk over my main ideas with you, but I do have plans for a very special garden which I'd love to be a surprise. The only problem is, you'd have to walk around blindfolded till it's completed and growing."

More laughter rumbled out of him. "I promise not to look too hard."

"That's going to be difficult since the garden will extend from the front of the villa to the sea."

"Then I'll drive around the back when I come in the house and refrain from letting my curiosity get the best of me."

"You'd actually do that?"

"You have my word."

She was inexplicably delighted by his willingness to go along with her.

"Then that's good enough for me."

"You've never been this amenable before. Greece must agree with you."

It does. Far too much, and all because of you.

Putting on a false smile she said, "It's because you're taking such perfect care of me, Perseus. Making a bargain with you is like making one with God. You never let down on your end." Her voice shook. "I just hope you feel you're getting your money's worth."

In an instant, the teasing rapport with him was gone. He rose from the lounger with a dark expression, towering over her like the god whose name he'd been given.

"We'll find out tonight when we pay a call on Sofia and her father."

Her heart lurched, and she had to fight to remain calm. "I'll do whatever you ask."

Silence reigned before he said, "That's a rash statement to fall from such innocent lips."

Her face felt hot.

"It's not rash at all," she countered. "You must have been desperate to have married me to help you deal with Sofia. After talking to her on the phone, I can see why. She was very penitent and convincing."

Sam swallowed over and over again. "I—it's entirely possible that after tonight, you won't need my services any longer."

"What in the name of heaven is that supposed to mean?" he thundered.

Mentally backing away from him she said, "Sofia is still in love with you, and she explained that there were reasons why she stabbed you before running away. Reasons that make sense if you'll only give her the chance to explain. When you hear her explanation, you may feel differently about everything a-and want to re-cap—"

"Enough—" he practically bellowed.

She shuddered because her comment seemed to have infuriated him even more.

"I've invested a considerable amount of money in you already, and expect you to remain loyal to me. Is that understood?"

"Yes, of course, Perseus. I wouldn't be anything else. I only meant that I'll understand if you two decide to get back together. You've already done so much for me, I could never repay you and wouldn't dream of holding you to the rest of our contract. If you and Sofia can resolve your differences, I'll be on the next plane back to New York."

He reached out and cupped her face in his hands. His body had grown rigid. "You won't be leaving to go anywhere until I tell you, you can go." As if to remind her of their pact, he lowered his mouth to hers and kissed her so hard and thoroughly, she felt dizzy.

"In any event," he murmured in thick tones minutes later, "it's a moot point since I'm in possession of your passport." After a tension-filled pause, "Everything you need to get started on the plans for our yard is sitting on the next table. If you desire anything else, I'll be in my study. *Me sinchorite*."

Upon excusing himself, he strode swiftly from the pool room and disappeared.

She stood there clinging to a chair, attempting to pick up the pieces of a conversation which had started out lighthearted, and had ended in a kiss that had rocked her to the very foundations.

The mention of Sofia had triggered a violent reaction in Perseus. Heartsick because when it was good with Perseus, she'd never been so happy in her life, she had a great deal of difficulty settling down to anything, let alone planning a yard of which he could be proud.

She had thought it was going to be a joint venture, but in pleading Sofia's case, she'd driven him away.

Lesson number one she said to herself, plopping a gardening catalog on her lap. Never collaborate with the enemy, not even with the best of intentions.

Sam would do well to remember that tonight when they went to the Leonidas's home. Sam wouldn't listen to anything Sofia had to say, nor would she go to Perseus about it.

When she thought about it, Perseus had every right to be upset with her. She'd let Sofia get to her, which was tantamount to betraying Perseus. Sam would never make such a mistake again.

Stung by his words and hurt over his departure, she plunged into her work as if a demon were in pursuit. At one point Ariadne made an appearance to clear away their brunch, but Sam hardly noticed the activity while she was sketching various designs.

The color schemes were already in her head. It was simply a matter of finding the plants which could survive the heat and do best in the island soil. Fortunately the catalogs Perseus had provided gave all the information she would need.

Several hours went by. Ariadne brought her a light lunch of grilled salmon and more luscious fruit. Of

Perseus, there was no sign. For all she knew he'd left the villa. He might even had asked Yanni drive him to the area where his helicopter stood ready to fly him to Athens for the day. She would never know, which caused another little pain to enter her heart.

Around three-thirty Sam decided to call it quits. She took everything back to her suite, pleased with what she'd accomplished, but now it was time to start thinking about the evening ahead.

There was one designer dress hanging in the closet which appealed to her immensely. It was a cream-colored *crepe de chine*, slim-fitting with short sleeves and a scooped neck. The simplicity of the style shouted elegance.

But if Sam chose to wear it, then the first thing she needed to do was get a little color. Being a New Yorker meant she was too pale. If she went swimming and stretched out on the sand for a while, she'd pick up some sun which would tint her cheeks and lighten the natural blond steaks in her hair.

Without wasting another moment, she slipped into her bikini, grabbed a towel and left her room through the sliding doors to run down to the water's edge.

In the far distance she spied several sailboats and a ferry. Otherwise, the line of the blue horizon was barely distinguishable where sky met water.

Slipping off her sandals, she ran into the aqua water, frolicked for a few minutes, then laid out on her towel to absorb the sun's burning rays. Though she was a true blonde, she had light olive skin and could tan well if she worked hard at it. But in this heat she'd have to be careful so she wouldn't burn.

Promising herself ten minutes, she closed her eyes and tried to rid her mind of everything troubling her. Slowly the peace and serenity of this heavenly spot, with the gentle lapping of water and a few gulls calling to each other overhead, lulled her into a light sleep.

"If you intended sabotaging tonight's outing, you're doing a good job," came a deep, accusing voice which jerked her awake and brought her to her feet in an instant.

"Perseus—" she cried, stepping away from him as soon as he'd shaken out the towel and draped it around her shoulders. She didn't know what bothered her more. His anger, or the sight and feel of his bronzed, well-honed body still dressed in cutoffs which rode low on his hips.

"I was only sunning myself for a few minutes."

"Twenty to be exact," he stated unequivocally. "Another few more and you'd be burned to toast. Come back to the house. *Now*."

She avoided his eyes, already aware of an unpleasant stinging on her midriff and upper thighs where the sun rarely touched her body. Slipping on her sandals, she followed in his footsteps. "I—I didn't realize. You have to believe me."

He paused mid-stride, his chest rising and falling as if he were having great difficulty controlling his disgust. "You're in Greece, not Central Park."

"I know that," she grumbled, hating it because he made her feel like a recalcitrant child.

"From now on, you'll inform either myself or Ariadne when you come down to the beach. And I'll extract another promise from you, as well. You'll never, ever go swimming alone."

"I promise," she said quietly when they reached the sliding door to her room. The fact that she wasn't a strong swimmer precluded her ever being that foolhardy. Unfortunately, Perseus didn't believe she had any common sense.

Wanting to change the subject she asked, ''What time should I be ready tonight?''

''I thought we'd leave here in an hour and drive to Panagia where you asked me if I lived. It overlooks the whole island. We'll have dinner in a quaint taverna I know you'll enjoy, then we'll go on to Livadi.''

Livadi was the port town which Perseus told her contained discos, bars and cinemas for the tourist crowd. His lack of enthusiasm for the place revealed his dislike of that kind of entertainment, or perhaps it was simply a cover for painful reminders of Sofia since she lived there with her father.

''Does an hour give you enough time?''

''Yes,'' she murmured, not wishing to say or do anything which would upset him further.

''There's lotion in the cabinet for your sunburn. If you put it on after your shower, it'll cut down on the pain.''

''Thank you,'' she whispered, wishing he wouldn't be so kind. It was getting harder and harder to remain objective and unaffected around him.

''I'll hurry.''

Without waiting for an answer, she stepped into the shower and shut the door, her heart pounding out of rhythm. Through the etched glass she saw him hesitate before he turned on his heel and left the bathroom. Only then did she remove her bikini and give her hair a good wash.

She didn't stay under the water long. Since she planned to wear her hair loose and flowing about her shoulders, she needed all the time possible to blow-dry the strands.

As Perseus had predicted, the aloe vera lotion did take some of the sting out of her sunburn. Luckily, her face hadn't burned to a lobster color yet, but anyone looking at her would recognize she'd had a healthy dose of sun.

The frosted coral lipstick she'd brought in her bag went well with her pinkish tan.

Strappy high heels in the same cream color as her dress completed her outfit. With a touch of *fleur de rocailles* French perfume he'd picked out for her, plus some expensive-looking gold hoops for her ears, she felt as ready as she'd ever be to accompany Perseus. Her only other adornment came in the form of her wedding ring.

The ring more than anything else made her feel a complete fraud. She'd taken it off after the ceremony, afraid to lose it. But she knew he'd expect it to be on her ring finger tonight, so she reached in the jewelry box and slid it home.

When she finally glanced in the mirror, a stranger stared back. It was herself, yet not herself. She looked elegant, sophisticated, polished and expensive. Her hair, lightened by the sun, had a tendency to curl and swung about her shoulders from a side part.

Right now it gleamed like gold—the perfect foil for Perseus Kostopoulos's dark good looks. Deep in her heart she was pleased that she wouldn't disappoint him.

When she recalled that first afternoon in his office-standing there drenched, with her scruffy hair pulled back with fishnet, and wearing that spotted denim shirt and jeans—she cringed to imagine what he must have thought.

Embarrassed by the memory, she turned to leave when she heard a knock on the adjoining door. "Samantha? May I come in?"

The breath all but left her body. "Y-yes. I'm ready." Then the door to his room opened and she found she was incapable of taking another.

This evening Perseus looked the ultimate male specimen, his broad shoulders aligned with a hard-muscled body clothed in a silky royal blue shirt and off-white trousers, a jacket of tiny blue pinstripes flung carelessly over his shoulder. His straight black hair had grown a little longer since the first day she'd met him, giving him a vaguely dangerous look.

He could easily be the heroic god he'd been named for, not only physically but in every other sense. As far as Sam was concerned, he was her hero. To this point in time she'd never seen him do anything unworthy. A magnificent man unchanged by his wealth and position.

His only flaw seemed to be that he was haunted by a past love, immobilizing him so that he couldn't move on with his personal life. A tragedy for the scores of women who would have desired a relationship with him.

But if Sam didn't miss her guess, Sofia would achieve her goal to be the *real, the one and only Mrs. Kostopoulos.*

One look at him tonight and Sofia would recognize that he was infinitely more desirable than the eighteen-year-old lover she'd adored in her heart all these years.

Sam had the strange premonition that their meeting tonight was going to change destiny, and she, Sam, would be given her freedom along with a bonus check for duties rendered.

The reality of that hurt more than any pain she'd ever suffered in her life, even the defection of her father and the death of her mother. Her eyes closed tightly. Every minute with Perseus had made her fall fathoms deeper in love with him.

Throughout all her silent emoting, she hadn't realized that Perseus had been standing there in pregnant silence, staring at her as if he couldn't believe what he was seeing. Had she worn the wrong outfit?

Feeling suddenly uncomfortable and restless, she inquired, "What is it? Why are you looking at me so strangely?"

"Come into the bedroom."

She blinked in shock.

His mouth quirked mockingly. "I want you to see something. I'm not about to seduce you. That was part of our contract."

Sam already despised their contract, and wished he'd never brought it up. Not able to imagine what he was getting at, she moved toward him on shaky legs. He was acting so mysterious. She felt him eye her progress with an intensity that sent a frisson of excitement across her skin.

When she reached him, he clasped her right hand and walked her the rest of the way into his room, leading her toward a large, framed, four-by-five foot painting which hung on the wall between the two double beds.

Of course. The painting of Andromeda. Sam had forgotten.

She stepped closer for a good look, then cried out in total shock, feeling the blood drain from her face.

"Perseus—" She swayed into him and he caught her against his chest, sliding his arms around her waist from behind so she wouldn't fall.

"Th-that's my mother!"

Sam's hair stifled the unintelligible words he said beneath his breath. "I knew there had to be an explanation for the likeness," his husky voice sounded at last. "Finally it all makes sense."

"What do you mean? I d-don't understand."

"Your beauty which has always been familiar to me. That spark of genius in your collage that sets you above everyone else."

Sam couldn't take any of this in. Not his amazing words, or the fabulous painting created by her father. A painting Perseus had bought years ago because he was so taken with the subject.

Her father *was* a genius. He'd caught her mother's

essence, her beauty, her young woman's body which was revealed beneath the diaphanous celadon-toned drape. It molded to every line and curve because of the ocean breeze. She was chained to a rock, her bare arms beckoning her beloved Perseus to save her from the sea monster.

Tears started gushing down her cheeks. "I've never seen my mother look so young, so bewitching. *Or so happy*! That's love light illuminating her face and eyes."

She fought for breath, and tried to control the rage that suddenly welled up inside her breast. "My father must have painted this before he left her alone and pregnant."

The room reverberated with the bitterness of her words, but she was helpless to recall them. They'd been dammed up too long.

On a little gold nameplate at the bottom of the frame she read, "My Andromeda." In the bottom right corner of the painting was her father's signature. *Jules*.

"*Dear God—*"

Unable to hold back any longer, she broke into a paroxysm of tears, instinctively turning her body to burrow against Perseus who held her against his heart for timeless moments, rocking her until the worst of her sobbing had subsided.

There was deep concern in his low, vibrant voice when he asked, "When was the last time you saw him, Samantha?"

She could hardly get the words out. "I—I've never seen him in person in my life, and I never want to. Please—never speak his name to me again. He doesn't exist for me."

Disgusted and ashamed because she'd broken down so completely in front of Perseus, she lifted her head and pulled free of his arms, avoiding his penetrating gaze.

"Forgive me for ruining your shirt. If you'll grant me

five minutes, I'll have fixed my makeup so we can go out to dinner.''

"We don't have to go anyplace.''

Trust Perseus to put her needs before his own. Another reason why her heart was breaking.

"Yes. Yes we do. Tonight is possibly the most important night of your life. I have a contract to fill and I intend to fulfill it. I'll meet you at the car.''

A few minutes later they left for Panagia, keeping to desultory conversation throughout their drive and meal. Finally, "Are you feeling ill?''

They were fast approaching Livadi and those were the first words Perseus had spoken since they'd left the *taverna*.

"No. Why do you ask that?''

His black brows knit together. "Because you only played with your food. I doubt one bite of octopus salad made it past your lips.''

He'd done everything to distract her by telling her amusing anecdotes, ordering native dishes she might otherwise never have had an opportunity to taste. Honorable to a fault, he'd refrained from mentioning her father or the scene at the villa. But she knew his innate concern for her welfare was troubling him.

Coming face-to-face with her mother's portrait, created by her absentee father, had been a tremendous shock, one he'd witnessed for himself. The problem was, Sam couldn't talk about it, not to anyone, particularly not Perseus who had demons of his own to exorcise. It would be unthinkable to add to his burdens.

She continued to stare out the passenger window so she wouldn't be tempted to feast her eyes on his distinctive, aquiline profile. Throughout dinner she'd grown increasingly aware of him. His economy of movement, the way he enjoyed his wine, the line of concentration between his brows when he was studying the menu.

Her mind doted on him continually. She'd memorized every adorable, wonderful, awesome, stern, reflective mannerism, especially the habit he had of absently rubbing his scar. The wound served as a part of the total man. But each time he made the gesture, Sam feared his anguished soul was remembering Sofia, longing for her.

If it meant he would stop thinking about her, she'd encourage Perseus to have it removed. To her mind, however, she wouldn't change one centimeter of him. He filled all the secret niches of her heart. He—

"We've arrived, Samantha. I give you my solemn oath you have nothing to worry about. Simply follow my lead."

She sucked in her breath and flashed him a bright, determined smile. "If I'm worried about anyone, it's you. I—" Her voice caught. "I realize you haven't seen her for twenty years. I just want you to know I'm praying for you."

He reached for her hand and kissed the palm, turning her bones to liquid. "Bless you," she heard him whisper in a husky tone.

The Leonidas villa was located in the heart of Livadi. The small, attractive dwelling built in Cycladic style Perseus explained, was chosen for its accessibility to the patients from town as well as the circle of islands for which the Cyclades had derived their name.

With one hand at her elbow, Perseus helped her from the car. Together they walked the short distance to the front door bordered by flowering bougainvillia.

"Kyrie Kostopoulos," a short, balding old man cried when he opened the door and saw Perseus. His leathery face was wreathed in a huge smile as the two men reached for each other and hugged. Soon the man was weeping, muttering rapid Greek into Perseus's ear. It warmed Sam's heart to witness such a happy reunion.

"Georgio, this is my wife, Samantha," he explained

in English for Sam's benefit she was sure. "Darling?" he said in a quiet aside, the endearment falling from his lips so naturally she couldn't countenance it. "Georgio has been with the Leonidas family for a good thirty years. He was one person who truly made me feel welcome here."

"I'm very happy to meet you, Georgio." Sam extended her hand which he shook with enthusiasm.

"Come in. Come in. The doctor is confined to his bed in the study now. This is not one of his good days, but he refuses to rest until he sees you. Sofia wishes a moment of your time first. You'll find her in the salon."

"Thank you, Georgio."

Whatever private thoughts were running through his head, Perseus gave no indication of his feelings. That superb control he possessed in abundance was in full evidence as he put a hand to her back and ushered her from the foyer to the next room which turned out to be an attractively furnished sitting room.

As soon as they had entered, Sam saw a tall, voluptuous, raven-haired woman step into the room from the other side. *Sofia.* Sam's thought was that she looked like a modern-day Carmen.

Though dressed in a tailored white, two piece suit, it seemed to emphasize her magnificent body and long tanned legs. She looked wildly exotic and utterly beautiful. She also looked like a woman who had suffered. Still, she was the kind of woman no man could ever forget...

Her liquidy black eyes didn't notice Sam. "*Perseus,*" she cried softly, all the love and longing she felt for him throbbing to life in that one word.

Suddenly a torrent of Greek broke from her lips, but Perseus bit out something else in kind which stopped her.

"Sofia." He spoke with such enviable calm, Sam was

staggered. "May I present my wife, Samantha. She doesn't speak a lot of Greek yet, but she's learning. Therefore I ask that you speak English in front of her."

The woman was obviously in pain. Sam could feel it, and she had it in her heart to feel sorry for her.

"How do you do," she murmured, but her eyes didn't leave Perseus's face. "I was hoping I might be able to talk to you in private. Please."

It took all Sam's strength not to turn to Perseus and beg him to grant Sofia that much.

"I'm married, Sofia." As if to emphasize that fact, he slid his hands over Sam's shoulders, squeezing gently. "My wife and I have no secrets from each other."

A wave of guilt assailed Sam, piercing her to the very core of her being because Sam had refused to confide in Perseus about her father.

"There's so much to say," the other woman lamented. "I hardly know where to begin. But before that, I have to beg your forgiveness." At this point the tears were rolling down her cheeks.

"I forgave you a long time ago, Sofia."

Again Sam marveled at his cool aplomb in the face of such a traumatic situation.

"I know there's no forgiveness for what I did. You're disfigured because of me. But at the time I had no choice. It was either that, or a bullet from my father's revolver to your heart."

"Spare the dramatics, Sofia."

"I don't blame you for not believing me. But twenty years ago, father's hatred of you and your father made him insane."

For the first time since they'd arrived at the house, something Sofia said pierced Perseus's armor. "What does my father have to do with this conversation?"

"You never knew that my father asked your mother to marry him before your father married her. But she turned him down because she was in love with your father.''

There'd be no reason for Sofia to make up such a story now. Sam believed her, and she had an idea Perseus did, too.

"Go on," he said in a voice that sounded as if it had come from an undersea grotto.

"It hurt his pride that she preferred a mere fisherman to an educated man who would one day be a doctor to the entire island. He married my mother because he needed a woman, but it was your mother he wanted.

"When Mother was killed by that bus, he never even grieved. After your father died at sea, your mother was all he could think about. He was getting ready to approach her when she became ill and you brought her to him. He considered her a gift from the gods, but he hated the very sight of you because you reminded him of your father.

"You were proud and strong. Very independent. And your fierce love for her was something he couldn't handle. I heard him making arrangements for you with Uncle Teo in Athens. He wanted you out of the house, but he swore me to secrecy.

"When we fell in love, he became violent. Spiros, down at the harbor, used to spy on us for him. He found out about the boat you'd hired to take us away to be married.''

Sam felt the shudder that passed through Perseus's powerful frame.

"When father found out what you were planning, he cornered me before I went to bed. He forbid me to see you again. He told me that if I didn't cooperate and send you away for good, he would kill you himself.''

A stillness came over Perseus. Sam could scarcely breathe.

"I was terrified. My father had always been insane

where you and your father were concerned. I didn't want you to die, and I was afraid he would carry out his threat. So I took his knife from his drawer and waited for you to come.

"I knew you would try to persuade me to go away with you, that I would have to do something terrible to make you leave me alone. But I swear I never meant to hurt you, Perseus. I never meant to." She broke down weeping. "I loved you more than life itself. I still do," she moaned in abject pain.

CHAPTER SEVEN

SAM tensed to leave the room. Perseus must have felt the change in her because his grip on her shoulders tightened until she almost cried out from the pressure.

Taking a long, shuddering breath Sofia said, "Father waited until you left the house, then he had me taken away to Turkey, and forced me to live in a convent. I was never allowed to leave. He provided for my keep, hoping that one day I'd become a nun. But I had no vocation and was kept there against my will.

"I eventually escaped and met a farmer who let me work for him. I had no passport, no money. I couldn't come back to Greece. When he offered me marriage, I accepted. He died six months ago, leaving me a small property which I sold so I could come back to Greece. But the authorities wouldn't allow me back in.

"In desperation I phoned the house and learned through Georgio that Father had been looking everywhere for me. He'd finally come to his senses, but it was too late. I'd fled the convent and left no traces.

"Georgio put Father on the phone. We talked, and he arranged for a new passport and passage. When I saw him again, I hardly recognized him because he was so ill. We've reconciled, but Father knows that what he did to you, to us, to me, was unforgiveable." Her voice shook.

"His life has been a living hell every day, every hour since I sent you away with that stab wound. I think the only reason he's still alive is because he must see you again and ask for absolution."

Perseus raked a hand through his midnight hair.

Perhaps no one else would notice, but Sam knew his every action and movement by heart. To her, it was a sign that Sofia's revelations had knocked the foundation of belief right out from under him.

"You mean to tell me that for the past twenty years, you've been in exile in Turkey?" he demanded in a barely controlled voice.

"Yes, Perseus. If you need proof, I can provide it."

His pained expression said everything. Sam had believed this night would change destiny, and she'd been right. Sofia had come home to Perseus. It wouldn't be long before the two star-crossed lovers were able to marry and find the happiness so long denied them. The pain of that reality was staggering.

"For your sake, I'll see him one last time. Samantha?" He kissed the top of her silken head. "Stay here. We won't be long. Would you like Georgio to bring you something to drink?"

"No, thank you." To her chagrin her voice trembled. "I'm fine. Please—take the time you need."

Subsiding into the nearest chair, she watched Perseus follow Sofia out of the room, the two of them moving in unison as if they'd never been apart.

Already Sam was forgotten. Which was as it should be.

Perseus hadn't known what he'd find when he saw Sofia again after all this time. That's why he'd used Sam for a shield. But now that shield was no longer necessary, and before long, Sam would be packing her bags. She'd served her purpose. When she left, Sofia would become the mistress of the Villa Danae.

No way was Sam going to help Perseus put in a garden now. As for expecting him to set her up in business, she wouldn't dream of holding him to that promise.

After listening to Sofia's horror story about her father, Sam no longer wanted revenge on her own parent. Jules

Gregory was a pathetic human being, but at least he hadn't interfered in her life, or caused her the kind of grief Sofia had been forced to suffer.

No. Tonight something had snapped inside Sam. The idea of trying to prove to her father that she'd done just fine without him held no appeal. It would be wasted emotion, wasted energy.

Perseus's life was a case in point. For twenty years he'd put his personal happiness on hold. As for Sofia, through no fault of her own, she'd lost as many years and had been forced to endure untold anguish. Sam was in danger of doing the same thing if she continued to entertain this vendetta against her father.

No. The anger had to end, and Sam was the only one who could end it, otherwise she'd be the loser.

While she sat there waiting, she made up her mind to leave Perseus in the morning. The purpose for which she'd come had been fulfilled. No reason existed to maintain the facade of nuptial bliss. Anyone with eyes could see that Perseus and Sofia belonged together. Sam didn't have any desire to stand in the way of their love a second longer than necessary.

In Sam's mind, she'd fulfilled her part of the contract. When she left, the clothes he'd given her would remain at the villa. She'd take nothing with her but the outfit she was wearing.

Since Perseus had spoiled her for all the other men in existence, she couldn't imagine marrying anyone else. Her only plan was to get as far away from Perseus and soul-destroying memories as possible.

Cheyenne, Wyoming, would fill the bill nicely. She had a great-aunt still living there. Her mother was buried there. It was a place to start. She'd get a job, and when she'd earned enough money, she'd pay Perseus back for all his help in getting her mother's body shipped to Wyoming and reburied.

She couldn't do anything about his gift to the art department at the university. He'd set up the fund, and would never renege on that pledge. However, Sam comforted herself that Perseus gave to many charities, and because he was an art lover, he wouldn't mind that some of his money had been channeled in that direction for deserving artists.

With her mind made up to let go of the anger harbored against her father, she found herself at peace for the first time in her life.

But the ache in her heart was another matter entirely. Sam was now in the torturous position of being the one who would go to the grave with Perseus's name on her lips…

Unable to remain there any longer, Sam decided to wait outside in the car for Perseus. The villa was quiet as a tomb as she tiptoed through the foyer and let herself out the front door.

A little sigh escaped as the warm, moist night air, heavy with the scent of hibiscus, immediately enveloped her. During the harsh Wyoming winters, when the blizzards raged and the air was so dry it turned the skin to paper, she'd miss Serifos desperately.

Approaching the car, she slumped against the passenger door for a moment, drained by Sofia's tragic story. The view of the blue Aegean Sea was always before her eyes, wherever she looked.

Look hard and long for the last time, Sam. Tomorrow you'll be winging your way to the Rocky Mountains, living more than a mile above sea level with no water in sight, let alone a mortal man who could ever compare to Perseus.

Suddenly a spate of unintelligible Greek met her ears. She straightened and whirled around to face the man who'd haunt her for the rest of her born days. His fierce expression caused her to wince. Somehow she'd supposed he would look quite different after his meeting with Sofia.

"I asked you to wait for me," he bit out. "What possessed you to leave without telling Georgio, at least?" His scar stood out white against the rest of his hard jaw.

She shook her head in bewilderment. His behavior didn't make any sense. "Since I had no idea how long you'd be, I came out here for a breath of fresh air," she explained, marveling that he'd react like this over something so trivial.

His body tautened. "As my wife, I expect you to act like one."

"But there's no longer any need to pretend in front of Sofia, Perseus. Now that you know the truth about what happened that day, everything has changed. The two of you have been reunited and deserve time alone to work out the rest of your lives. Tomorrow I'm taking the morning ferry back to Athens, then fly home to the States."

Darkness had settled over the island, so maybe it was the twinkling of the harbor lights which made her think for an infinitesimal moment that his expression had lost its animation.

In a lithe movement, he opened the passenger door and told her to climb in. She gladly complied since she couldn't get away to the privacy of her own room and thoughts fast enough. They drove in absolute silence at a speed only someone born to the island, someone who knew its every curve and climb, would have dared maintain.

Taking Sam back to the villa when he wanted to stay with Sofia was probably the hardest thing he'd ever had to do. But being the total gentleman, he would see to Sam's needs first, then return to Livadi to work out the rest of his life. A life Sam would have no part of.

She gripped her hands together in anxiety. How she wished she'd never met Sofia!

No wonder another woman had ever been able to attract Perseus! At thirty-eight, Sofia was at the height of her beauty. Those huge, dark, soulful eyes staring at him with naked adoration must have gone a long way to heal his pain and suffering. A night in her arms would take care of the rest. And the thousands of nights thereafter...

Sam couldn't bear the pictures that kept flashing through her mind, but she had no place to run with her pain. She was forced to sit there and clamp down hard on the new emotions exploding inside her without giving anything away to Perseus. Because these feelings were so new and raw, she didn't know how to deal with them.

When the car pulled up to Perseus's villa ten minutes later, she alighted from the front seat unaided. Right now she needed to be alone with her pain.

"Where do you think you're going?" He moved with the speed of a panther and caught up with her, catching hold of her wrist in a firm grip, preventing her from taking another step.

"In the house, of course," she retorted, her panic rising because his physical nearness was creating havoc with her senses.

"Earlier you said you wanted some fresh air. I find I'm in need of it, too." He started taking off his shoes and socks.

Her eyes grew huge as she looked down at his dark head. "But Sofia is waiting for you to return, and—"

"Sofia's father is on the verge of death," he inserted in a low, sober tone. "The priest is probably with them as we speak."

She swallowed hard, trying to imagine his pain because the long-awaited reunion with Sofia would have to be put off out of reverence for her dying parent.

Moistening her lips nervously she asked, "W-was it

unbearable having to face her father? Did he own up to what he'd d—"

"Let's just say Sofia was telling the truth," Perseus broke in evenly before she could emit another word. "To answer your next question…" He read her mind with astonishing ease. "We made our peace. Now that's the end of it."

So saying, he set his things on the sand and once again got down on his haunches, this time in front of her.

"What are you doing?" she cried out in shock.

"Removing your shoes so you can walk along the beach with me."

Of necessity, she had to cling to his powerful shoulders so she wouldn't fall over. The touch of his fingers brushing her slim ankles sent waves of delight through her body.

"But, Perseus? I thought—"

"You think too much, Kyria Kostopoulos." Again he'd cut her off without so much as an excuse me. "Do you need help with your hose?"

White-hot heat suffused her face. "Of course not! If you'll turn around, I—I'll remove them."

She heard a wicked chuckling sound before he tossed his jacket next to his shoes with unconscious male grace and started walking toward the gentle surf.

Because Sam's whole being shook with repressed excitement as well as confusion, she was all thumbs as she lifted the hem of her dress and managed to peel the confining material from her hips and legs.

Wadding her hose into a little ball, she tucked it inside one of her shoes, then turned to join Perseus who stood watching her approach. With his feet planted apart in the foam, he looked like the powerful god of his namesake.

In the darkness, it was impossible to discern the look on his face. But even if she could see his expression, the enigmatic mask he presented to the world would be in place, hiding the real Perseus.

"Come." He held out his hand. In that one simple word she felt some unnamed emotion that compelled her to grasp it. No matter how strong he was, how in control of every situation, she knew that his seeing Sofia had come as a tremendous shock.

More than likely he needed Sam's companionship because she was the one person who knew the truth. She'd already displayed that she was sensitive to his needs. He could count on her not mistaking his attentions for anything more than friendship, albeit a strange one based on a contract which, after tonight, would no longer be in effect.

They continued walking through the shallow water beyond the point where they could see the lights from the villa before. When she couldn't stand it any longer she blurted, "Sofia is very beautiful."

He sucked in his breath, but didn't pause in his stride which he'd paced to suit hers. "There are differing kinds of beauty. Certainly Sofia has a bewitching quality many men would find provocative."

Sam's heart was in her throat, but she had to ask and knew he needed to talk about it. "Was it hard seeing her again?"

"Yes." His voice grated. "She's no longer eighteen. Life has brought irrevocable changes, and one can never go back."

He sounded so haunted, she could have wept. "That's true, but you're both still young enough to have a brilliant future. You can be married right away and start a family."

"That would be impossible."

"Of course it's not!" she fired back. "Tomorrow I'll sign whatever I have to sign to give you your freedom."

His hand seemed to tighten around hers, as if he were in the throes of intense emotion.

"That isn't the issue, Samantha. Even if her father passes away in the next few days, the period of mourning lasts a long time here on the island."

Her eyes fluttered closed out of pain for him. "You've waited twenty years. How cruel to be separated for even a few more weeks."

"More like fifty-two."

Her eyes flew open. "What?"

At her outcry, he came to a standstill and faced her. "Decency would compel Sofia to wait a year, at least."

Her body shook with outrage. "It would be indecent to make either of you wait that long after what has transpired!"

"Nevertheless, it's the Greek way, and we're both traditionalists. None of us involved could afford the inevitable gossip. Therefore you're going to have to remain my faithful wife until the time comes that I can claim my heart's desire."

To live with him for a whole year, but never really live with him? It was unthinkable. She couldn't do it!

Sam pulled her hand free of his. Out of the corner of her eye she detected a grimace darkening his features.

"Is the thought of a year with me so abhorrent to you?"

"No!" she cried, shaking her head. "Of course not. I'm only thinking of *you*. How painful it's going to be living on the same island, knowing she's only a few minutes away, yet not being able to go to her—love her—" Her voice wobbled precariously. Feeling his anguish, her head flew back. "Does she know about us?"

His black gaze impaled her. "She knows how I feel, so that there can be no mistake, no misunderstandings."

"Y-you're sure she doesn't hate me?"

"Can anyone know what is in another person's heart?" he asked silkily.

"It's enough that I have told her the truth. How she deals with that truth is for her to handle, and is of no concern to you."

By now Sam was a jumbled mass of feelings. "If I were Sofia, no matter what I knew intellectually, I couldn't bear to see you living with another woman. I-It would kill me. I'd be in such hell, I'd want to scratch the other woman's eyes out!"

An unexpected smile started at the corner of his mouth and widened until it reached his eyes. He looked years younger and so attractive, she almost fainted at the sight.

"Such violent emotion..." His deep voice trailed. "Fortunate indeed would be the man who inspired that kind of passion." His hand suddenly lifted to his scar. "While we're on the subject of violence, I thought I'd fly to Athens next week to see about having this removed."

The change of subject, let alone his intentions, stunned Sam. Only Sofia could have inspired that decision.

Feeling inexplicably hurt, she started walking back the way they'd come, not caring if she splashed water on the hem of her dress. He wasn't far behind.

"If you're worried about being left alone, you're welcome to come to Athens and stay at the apartment while I have the surgery."

She could feel her anger kindling. "In case you didn't notice, I'm a big girl now, Perseus, and have lived alone for a long time."

"Actually I *did* notice," he came back with aggravating persistence. "So what you're really saying is that when we made our contract, you hadn't counted on playing nursemaid."

"You're deliberately misunderstanding me."

"If that's so, then explain to me why my decision to have the scar removed has upset you so much."

"It hasn't upset me!" She hurried faster to put distance between them.

"Then why don't you stop running away."

His challenge made her feel foolish and she slowed her steps.

"Look at me, Samantha."

She didn't want to look at him. He might see the same love light in her eyes which had been captured in the painting of her mother. Then Perseus would know everything...

"If you're afraid for me, you don't have to be. Modern plastic surgery can do miraculous things with a minimum of discomfort." He spoke in a low, soothing tone.

"I know that." Her voice actually squeaked.

"Then what's troubling you? I'll get the answer if we have to stay here all night."

She reached for a little shell jutting out of the sand. "What you do is your own business, Perseus. Naturally Sofia hates it because it's a brutal reminder of what she did to you."

After a slight hesitation, "I was just going to say that I—I can't imagine you without it. I've had to take some sculpting classes, and it's my belief that the statues critically acclaimed to be the most beautiful by the worlds' art connoisseurs, generally miss being truly magnificent because they have no flaw that sets them apart and makes them unique."

The second the words left her lips, a pulsating stillness emanated from him.

Only then did she realize that she'd spoken out of turn once more, and had all but told him he was physically perfect to her. Right now she could wish there were a sea monster who would drag her to his underwater grotto so she wouldn't have to face Perseus again.

"I wonder if you would be so brave if we didn't have a contract."

She whirled around, furious. "The contract has nothing to do with anything. There isn't a woman alive who wouldn't find you attractive, Perseus."

The air throbbed between them.

"Then prove it. Forget we have a contract, and show me you wouldn't wince from such a disfiguration."

Perseus might be all man, but for an instant, his words reminded her of a proud little boy who'd rather die than admit he was afraid of rejection. Sam had no defense against that kind of appeal, and found herself moving toward him.

Without conscious thought she lifted her hands to his face and raised on tiptoe to kiss his scar, not once, but many times because she loved him more than she'd thought it possible to love another human being.

A torrent of Greek words broke from Perseus's lips, then his mouth found hers, driving the breath from her body. They were melded together, moving and breathing as one flesh. Sam forgot everything in the rapture of being in his powerful arms like this and held nothing back, giving him kiss for kiss.

Then just as unexpectedly, the ecstasy stopped. Perseus pushed her away from him, as if he'd come to the sudden, shocking realization that he'd been kissing the wrong woman.

He walked on ahead of her to pick up their things off the sand. Sam followed a little ways behind, her heart sore with a brand-new ache.

Obviously the experiment had worked. She'd proven to him that his scar had nothing to do with his magnificent looks or potent sexuality. But in the proving, she'd set up the means of her own destruction.

In the days that followed, she lived to regret her impulsive action of taking up his dare. No matter that they had a business arrangement, she couldn't forget that he'd opened up a new world of sensual joy to her.

In Sam's eyes what they'd done the other night constituted a mockery of the supposedly sacrosanct state of marriage. Worse, she found it almost unbearable to revert to a platonic relationship each time they found themselves alone with each other.

Hard work was her only salvation, and right now she disliked being interrupted while she was supervising the men delivering the topsoil. Since her arrival, the sprinkling system had been put in, probably the only one of its kind on the island. Another day or two and everything would be ready for planting.

"Kyria Kostopoulos? The phone!" Ariadne shouted from the doorway. Most likely it was another business call for Perseus. There'd been quite a few of them because he'd taken off more time from his work to help Sofia with her father's funeral arrangements and burial. Throughout the proceedings, he'd insisted that Sam be at his side, carrying on in her role as beloved wife while they were under the scrutiny of his fellow islanders.

Since Sam adored Perseus to the last tiny cell of her body, the part came as naturally to her as breathing. Too naturally. She welcomed his open display of affection, savored every kiss, every caress calculated to impress people that they were honeymooners who couldn't keep their hands off each other.

But there was a down side to playing such a dangerous game. While poor Sofia had to stand by and watch in frozen silence, Sam was required to follow Perseus's amorous lead, fully realizing that beneath this loving charade, he was counting the hours until he had the legitimate right to be in the other woman's arms.

"Can you take the message?" she shouted back.

"It's your husband!"

Perseus.

He'd left for Athens early that morning by helicopter, ostensibly to catch up on work at his office. But she had the gut feeling he'd been to see the plastic surgeon. If he'd opted to have an operation, then he'd probably decided to stay over and was calling to inform her.

The disappointment of knowing he'd planned to go ahead without telling her his intentions, let alone that he wouldn't be home tonight, almost incapacitated her. She dreaded hearing bad news, but there was nothing to do except hurry into the house so she wouldn't keep him waiting any longer than necessary.

Since that night on the beach, not another word had been mentioned about his scar, or the woman he loved. It was as if such a moment had never happened.

During the last few days he'd fallen into a pattern of breakfasting with her around the pool while they discussed plans for the yard. On a couple of occasions, he'd declared that they'd done enough work. After asking Maria to prepare a picnic for them, he'd driven Sam to various points of interest on the island so she could play tourist.

And always at night, he insisted that they take an evening swim in front of the villa before going to bed. Those were the moments of agony and ecstasy, cavorting in the waves with Perseus, then floating on the velvet sea while he made lazy circles around her with one powerful sweep of his arm. His touching stories about his youth made her want to laugh and cry at the same time.

Slowly she found herself recalling past incidents, particularly life at the university, the characters she'd met in the art department.

But Perseus didn't let it stop there. He had a way of getting her to talk about growing up in New York, about her mother.

Little by little, as she grew more comfortable around him, he drew out memories so deeply buried, she'd forgotten they were there…especially those childhood fears over her mother's poor health.

On that point, Sam and Perseus shared similar remembrances. He, too, had worried about his mother's anemia, and therefore understood Sam's subsequent insecurity.

In all ways but one, Sam had never been happier in her life. Each day was like a fantastic dream that grew more wonderful with the passage of time. She'd only known him a little less than a month, yet already she felt inexplicable joy just to be alive.

How in heaven's name would she survive a permanent separation after living with him a full year?

The answer was simple. She wouldn't…

No matter Perseus's declaration that she must stay with him until Sofia's period of mourning had passed, Sam couldn't go on this way much longer. She couldn't take any more nights in the water where her physical awareness of him had grown too acute.

He could have no conception of how her body burned from the slightest contact with his. She experienced literal pain each time he bundled her up in a beach towel and laughingly carried her back to the villa so she wouldn't track sand in the house.

"Perseus?" She fought to keep a level tone after speaking into the receiver.

"You sound out of breath." His deep voice reached out to grab at her emotions.

"I was talking to the foreman about putting in one more layer of soil before the day is out."

"Try to finish up soon. I'm sending the helicopter for you."

Her heart lurched painfully. "Does this mean you're going into the hospital?"

A brief silence ensued. "No, Samantha. You decided me against having the surgery."

"I did?" she cried out in shock, pleased beyond words that she had any influence over him at all. "But I thought—"

"As I told you before," he interrupted suavely, "you think too much for your own good. I've decided it's time we had a night out in Athens. You were too tired to enjoy it before. Wear something dressy. I'll be waiting for you when you arrive at eight."

Her emotions were in such turmoil, she bit her lip and tasted blood. "Perseus—th-there's nothing I'd like more, but I guess the heat has gotten to me today. I felt a headache coming on after lunch, and even with some tablets, it still hasn't gone away completely," she lied without any compunction. "Would you mind if we went out another time?"

There was a dramatic silence on the other end. "Under the circumstances I'd be more upset if you didn't take care of yourself. I'll be home soon."

"No!" She twisted the phone line so hard she pinched a finger, causing her to wince. *Don't come near me tonight.* "There's no reason. Stay in Athens and enjoy yourself, visit with friends you haven't seen for a long time."

No doubt there's a woman who has missed your company and will be overjoyed to have you to herself for a little while.

"You insult me by suggesting I have a pillow friend," he rasped with a harshness in his tone she hadn't heard since that first day in his office. Not only that, he'd read her mind with uncanny perception.

"Contrary to world opinion, not every man in Greece is unfaithful to his wife. We're married, Samantha. I made vows which I intend to honor. Expect me within the hour." The line went dead.

CHAPTER EIGHT

SAM shivered from his curtness, almost dropping the receiver in the process. He was angry. Really angry.

Realizing she didn't have much time, she dashed out of the house to tell the foreman to finish up. Then she hurried back inside for her shower, informing a concerned Ariadne that she wasn't feeling well, so she was going to skip dinner and go straight to bed.

Though Sam hadn't had a sign of a headache when she'd answered the phone, she'd developed one since talking to Perseus. Hopefully a couple of pills would help her to fall asleep before he could make it back to the island.

She couldn't understand why he'd become so upset. In the eyes of the law they might be legally wed, but they weren't really married!

He had every right to be with whatever woman he desired. Perhaps on the island he had to be discreet. But in Athens, surely there would be no problem spending time with a girlfriend of long association. Sam could never blame him for seeking feminine comfort until he and Sofia were finally married.

But Perseus had an honorable streak that ran deep. As long as he and Sam had been through a legal ceremony, he obviously intended to remain true to their nuptials. As for her being sick, he would cancel everything to put her needs before his, because that was the way he was made.

If she could be sound asleep by the time he arrived, he wouldn't have to play nursemaid to her, and could make use of the free time working on new business ventures.

Closing the shutters against the early evening light, she climbed under the covers and turned on her stomach, burying her face in the pillow. Hopefully by the time Yanni had driven Perseus back from the helipad, she'd be in that necessary state of oblivion.

Ah, if wishes could become reality. Under normal circumstances, she might have relaxed enough to fall asleep early. But such wasn't the case. In fact this evening her senses seemed extra perceptory. She found herself listening to every sound, and locked on to the low purring noise of the car engine long before it pulled into the drive. Perseus was home.

Unfortunately her heart began its sickening pounding. Soon the blood echoed the same beat in her ears until she was a writhing mass of conflicting emotions. Part of her rejoiced he was back safely from Athens. The other part trembled for fear of getting too close to him. One of these days she was going to give herself away completely. Something had to be done to prevent that from happening...

Soon she heard men talking outside. Since the workmen had gone home for the night, the voices had to belong to Yanni and Perseus. Evidently he was making comments to the older man about the amount of work accomplished in the garden since morning. Sam had an idea he'd be pleased at the progress.

But in that assumption she was wrong. Totally wrong.

Moments after their voices had faded, she heard footsteps in the hall, and then the door to her room opened. Perseus had never come into her room without knocking first, but she imagined that Ariadne had told him Sam had been in bed for a while, so he'd decided to check up on her without making a disturbance. She thought of course he'd go away again.

To her consternation he came all the way in and shut the door, returning the room to its former near-darkness. The next thing she knew, he'd moved to the side of the bed. She felt the back of his hand against the part of her sunburned face not buried in the pillow.

He muttered something in low, unintelligible Greek, and suddenly the lights went on. Sam gasped and lifted her head, only to face the blazing anger of obsidian-black eyes.

"No wonder you've got a headache!" he thundered. "I warned you to wear a hat when you worked in the sun. Don't you know how dangerous it is to expose your skin like that? I leave you alone for a day and look what has happened to you." He sounded livid, but she heard the underlying concern. It wasn't something he could feign.

She sat straight up in the bed. Because she'd lied about a headache, she'd upset him needlessly. If she'd known it was going to produce this reaction, she would never have turned down the invitation to join him in Athens.

"It's only a minor sunburn, Perseus." She tried to placate him in a cajoling tone. "I usually get it at the beginning of the summer. From then on, I tan."

"To damnation with a tan. A woman's skin should be one of her most prized possessions. *You* have the kind of dewy complexion most women would kill for."

She blinked, having no idea he'd ever even noticed. Another memory to cherish.

"When we met, you weren't wearing makeup. Obviously you don't need it. Because you're so blessed, it would be criminal to abuse your skin. Whatever you've done in the past, while you're married to me you'll take care of yourself, even if it means you don't work in the yard anymore."

By now she was clutching the lapels of her white silk,

sleeveless pajama top to her neck. Not out of fear— Not for any other reason than because no one had ever worried about her welfare before, not even her mother who'd loved her desperately. For Perseus to pamper her like this was an unaccustomed luxury.

She hated it when he was unhappy, especially if she was the cause of it. Heavens, he'd been so wonderful to her!

"I admit it was foolhardy to stay out in the sun so long without protection. I promise to wear the hat from now on."

He studied the earnest expression on her upturned face for several seconds, testing the veracity of her words. "Ariadne tells me you went to bed without any dinner. You at least need to drink something so you won't get dehydrated."

She nodded. "You're right." If the truth be known, she was ravenous.

"Are you up to a crushed ice fruit drink?"

"Actually, that sounds exactly like what the doctor ordered. It will probably help my headache."

His eyes narrowed on her mouth, reducing her to a quivering lump of desire held barely in check. "Let's hope so. I'll be right back."

To her relief his initial black mood had lightened a little. It was up to her to get them back on a normal footing. Giving him something to do for her helped the process along.

In no time at all he'd returned, an iced peach drink in his hand. She had an idea he'd whipped it up himself, and loved him all the more for it.

"Thank you," she whispered when he handed it to her. She took care that their fingers didn't brush against each other. When his mouth thinned ominously, she didn't know if she'd offended him again or not.

"Drink every drop. You need the liquid." He was gone before she could wish him good-night.

Wide-awake, she sank back against the cushions and sipped her drink. Not one word had been mentioned about the yard, or his day at work. She wondered if he'd found it refreshing or hectic to be back at his office. Tonight there'd be no dip in the sea with him so she could find out, she lamented mournfully.

When she'd drained the delicious contents, she got out of bed and padded over to the shutters to open them. The tile felt cool beneath her bare feet. For a moment she stood looking at the view of the water where she'd spent some of the happiest hours of her life with Perseus, then she went over by the connecting door to flick off the light switch.

Just as the room darkened, the door opened. "Perseus—" she gasped softly when he suddenly appeared in the aperture, dressed in a belted, dark brown robe. She'd seen his chest bare when they'd gone swimming. But the sight of him dressed as he was somehow made everything more intimate. The dark, attractive, virile picture he made stole her breath.

"I was just about to shut off the light for you. How's the headache?"

She couldn't concentrate this close to him, let alone answer. His compelling masculinity was too overpowering for that. The darkness seemed to exaggerate the raw tension between them. Her only thought was to hide. Slowly she backed away and slid beneath the covers of her bed.

"Apparently it's worse than I thought," came the grim comment. "Turn on your side and I'll massage your neck for a few minutes. Sometimes it helps me when I'm in pain."

"It's all right, Perseus. I—I don't—"

"I'll decide what you require, and what you don't."

The hint of authority in his tone kept her silent. She should have fought him harder, but he'd already lowered himself on top of the covers behind her. When he moved a swathe of long, golden hair away from her neck, she felt electrified.

At the first magic touch of his fingers, the sensation was so heavenly, she thought she'd die right there. If she was feeling any pain, it was a surfeit of ecstasy.

For a while she felt his hand caress her neck up into her hair, then he slid it down to her shoulder, half covered by her top. He knew exactly where to apply pressure, where to rotate his fingers for maximum pleasure.

"Oh, that feels divine." She couldn't prevent the little moan that escaped.

"It's supposed to."

A huge lump lodged in her throat. "Between the drink you made me, and the rubdown, my headache has gone. You're too good to me, Perseus. There's no way I can repay you."

His hand stilled on her neck. "I don't want repayment, Samantha," came the husky rejoinder. "That implies owing something for services rendered. What I want has to be given freely, or not at all."

He was thinking of Sofia, of course. At the end of her mourning period, she'd be free to love him the way he needed to be loved. More than anything in life Sam wished she were the woman Perseus wanted. But that wasn't meant to be. None too soon his comment had brought her back to stark reality.

"I—I'm feeling so much better, why don't you turn on your other side and I'll try to relieve some of your tension. I would imagine your first day back at work wasn't all joy."

"How perceptive of you," he drawled in amusement before responding to her suggestion. She thought of course he'd be off the bed by now, wishing her good-night. Instead he had stretched out beside her like a great jungle cat. Most likely he was the one with the headache, but he'd never let on. This brought out her compassionate instincts and she rolled toward his back, wanting to soothe him for a change.

"Is your Athens office as spotless as the one in New York? Do you have another Mrs. Athas who takes care of your billion-dollar clutter?"

"It is, and I do," he muttered in a deep, gravelly voice, already sounding drugged as she massaged his neck the same way he'd massaged hers. His muscles were taut. He needed relief. "Perseus—lie flat on your stomach and I'll give you a back massage. When mother became ill, I used to give her one every night."

"What about your headache?"

"I told you. It's gone. Let this be my gift to you. It's free, and I want to do it."

"Then I accept." The low chuckle that rumbled out of him warmed her heart. He turned his magnificent body so he was hugging the bed, but his face was turned away from her.

He would receive more benefit if she asked him to remove his robe, but he hadn't taken it off, and she didn't dare suggest it, so it stayed.

"You're right," he said in a slurred voice after a few minutes. "What you're doing is divine. Don't ever stop."

"I won't," came her fervent reply. This was the closest she would ever come to worshiping his body. She would do it all night if he'd allow it.

As it turned out, within twenty minutes he was making the sounds of a person in a deep sleep. The poor darling was exhausted, physically and emotionally.

She started to ease herself off the bed when a strong hand snaked out to grasp her arm, preventing movement.

"Don't leave me," he muttered. "I don't want to be

alone tonight, *Kyria*.'' Before she knew how it happened, the top half of his body had covered hers. ''Show me once more you don't mind my scar,'' he begged in a husky voice.

Though she'd promised herself never to let this happen again, Sam had no defense against such importuning and gave up her mouth to him. If for these few minutes he was pretending that Sam was Sofia, it didn't seem to matter. The hunger of his passion broke down every feeble barrier she'd tried to erect, and she was lost.

''Perseus—'' she cried out helplessly as their kisses became more frenzied and feverish.

Calling out his name must have made him realize he'd been making love to the wrong woman. Before she could countenance it, he'd torn his lips from her creamy shoulder, and had levered himself from the bed, his breathing tortured.

''You've surpassed yourself in the acting department. Have no fear that I'll never ask you to prove yourself on that point again.'' In the next breath, he'd disappeared.

Like a wounded animal, she lay back down, unable to move. Immediately the faint scent of the soap he used assailed her senses. It was on the sheets, the pillowcase. The next best thing to being in Perseus's arms was to lie here and dream of him until morning. Such a little sin, one she prayed God would forgive.

When she awakened the next morning, the clock on the bedside table said ten-fifteen, and the room was filled with light. At that point, recollections of what had happened last night flooded her system.

She threw off the covers and jumped out of bed, anxious to see if Perseus was still asleep in his bed. But when she poked her head around the door, all she saw was his unmade bed with the blanket tossed aside. Perseus had gone without disturbing her.

Was he outside working?

She quickly dressed in shorts and a T-shirt. Donning her sandals, she hurried out of the house and ran around the villa hoping to catch sight of him.

The workers paused in their job of preparing the flower beds for planting and waved to her. She reciprocated, but her frustration grew because Perseus was nowhere in sight.

Retracing her steps, she almost collided with Ariadne who'd just stepped into the foyer.

By now she was out of breath. "Have you seen Perseus?"

"Yes. He was up early and left for Athens. He asked that you call him the moment you awakened."

She'd never had a reason to call him in Athens. "Do you have his number?"

"Yes, Kyria Kostopoulos. Come to the study with me."

Sam followed her into the clearly masculine room where Perseus conducted business when he couldn't be at his office. There was a large mahogany desk, bookcases filled with a plethora of various titles, a fax machine, copier, computer and printer. Everything he needed at his fingertips.

"I've written it down for you."

"Thank you, Ariadne," she said as the other woman left the room. Once she was alone, she picked up the receiver to punch in the numbers. When the secretary on the other end answered, Sam's ears met with a spate of rapid Greek.

Sam asked if the woman spoke English, and instantly his secretary reverted to perfect English. Sam couldn't help but be impressed and promised herself that one day her Greek would be as good as that woman's English. So far she'd been trying to say as many things in Greek as she could, but it was slow work.

"Kyria Kostopoulos—your husband said you would be calling. Please hold the line and I'll put you through to him."

"Thank you."

No matter how many times people referred to him as her husband, she would never get used to it because he *wasn't* her husband. Otherwise they would have spent last night in the same bed, and all the rest of their nights, forever!

"Samantha? You're up." He sounded vital, like he felt good. Apparently with a sound sleep, his little lapse last night had been completely forgotten, destroying her secret hope that he'd been as affected by their passionate interlude as she had.

"W-why didn't you waken me?" Her question came out sounding smothered.

"Because this morning the foreman told me you've been working harder than his own crew. That's probably the reason you were ill yesterday. He says you deserve a rest, and I happen to agree with him. How are you feeling? Is your headache gone?"

"Y-yes. I feel fine." He had her tongue-tied.

"I'm glad to hear it since I'm going to reissue my invitation to take you dining and dancing in Athens tonight. I want you to spend the rest of the day making yourself beautiful. I'll send the helicopter for you at seven. Yanni already has his instructions to drive you to Livadi."

Though terrified by the invitation because every moment spent in his company increased the depth of her feelings for him, she couldn't refuse him a second time.

"I'll be ready."

"We won't be coming back until tomorrow night, so pack an overnight bag."

Excitement passed through her body. "Where will we be staying?"

"Let that be my surprise. Until tonight." He murmured a word she didn't understand before he hung up.

Sam shouldn't have been so eager. This was wrong. But to defy him at this point would be an outright betrayal of him and everything she stood for. Somehow she had to start viewing him as a dearly beloved brother, or she wouldn't get through the next eleven months. But she didn't have the faintest idea how to go about doing that.

The clock on the wall said it was only ten-thirty in the morning. Since she had an idea Perseus wouldn't like it if she overdid it in the yard today, she refused to risk his displeasure a second time.

Instead, she'd take the sedan parked in the garage and drive to Hora, the fairy-tale town Perseus had told her about with its Venetian castle. He'd assured her that the car was there for her use. It would be good to get out of the house, away from everything that reminded her of him.

She could have lunch at a *taverna* before driving on to Galani. Apparently there was a fortresslike monastery near the village which housed some exquisite wall paintings and important illuminated manuscripts. She'd love to see those.

Then before returning to the villa, she'd have time to drive into Livadi to do a few errands and inspect the local pottery. Just two days before, Perseus had reminded her that as soon as the yard was done, he would introduce her to the manager of the local textile plant. Whenever she said the word, she could be put to work plying the craft she loved best.

It didn't seem possible that in the near future, her own designs would be marketed to an ever-increasing tourist trade. That day couldn't come soon enough for Sam.

With Perseus flying between New York and Athens, and her attempting to fill every waking hour at the plant with work, they wouldn't be able to spend nearly as much time together. The less, the better! Maybe under those conditions she could last until Sofia's mourning period was over.

Feeling somewhat reassured, Sam got ready for her outing. Aware that as long as she was Perseus's wife, she would always be a target for photographers, she put on a sensible pair of white cotton pants any tourist might wear, and toned them with a sage-green cotton top.

To keep the hair out of her face, she pulled it back in a French twist. Once she'd donned sunglasses and favorite walking shoes, she informed Ariadne she was leaving.

As a concession to Perseus, she took along the straw hat he'd bought for her to wear in the garden. It would come in handy when the sun reached its zenith, and disguise her hair.

Knowing Perseus as she did, she left her itinerary with the housekeeper, in case he called for some unexpected reason and demanded to know where she'd gone.

Sam was starting to learn a few of his ways. Because of his need to protect the people he cared about, he came across as angry when he thought something was threatening their welfare. The longer she lived with him, the more she was aware of this pattern developing. She had no desire to see Ariadne get into trouble because of negligence on the part of her employer's wife.

The outing started out well enough. Equipped with a map Ariadne had found for her, Sam made her way to the castle town with its adorable cube-shaped houses clustered in island style, delighting her artistic eye.

The food at the quaint café near the castle was equally enjoyable. Phyllo dough wrapped around beef slices, feta, bacon and hard-boiled egg. Replete from her meal, she drove on to Galani and marveled at the monastery's art treasures.

But it became clear to her that no matter how wonderful everything appeared to be, without Perseus to share it, nothing really mattered. Like salt which had lost its savor, a day without his vital, living presence was little more than a survival test in human endurance. She'd failed it miserably. By the time she reached Livadi, her heart had already picked up speed just anticipating her reunion with Perseus.

In a hurry to get home now, she bought a few necessary toiletries, then left the shop, intent on returning to her car without having her picture taken.

She hated the idea that people were following her. In the other villages, she'd been pretty well left alone. But here in Livadi, people recognized her and tried to get shots of her.

One dark-blond man of medium height, who appeared to be in good shape considering he was probably in his late fifties, had been dogging her footsteps since she'd gone into that shop.

Furious at him, she started to run, hoping to lose him. When she rounded the corner where her car was parked, her hat fell off. She stooped to pick it up, and that was when she heard him call out, "Samantha Telford? Is that you?"

He was an American. More to the point, he'd just called her by her maiden name. But if he was a newspaper reporter, then he had access to all the information he could ever want where she was concerned. Still, she slowed to a brisk walk and looked back over her shoulder. He was wearing sunglasses, too.

"Do I know you?" she snapped.

"No."

His one word reply surprised her.

"Then I have nothing to say."

Without further ado, she sprinted toward the car and unlocked the door. He was right behind her. "But I do.

In fact I have so much to say, I don't know where to start. You're going to have to help me. I'm your father, Jules Gregory.''

Sam froze in place.

The possibility of coming face to face with the man who'd gotten her mother pregnant—the man Sam had made up her mind she never wanted to meet in this lifetime, or the next—seemed too great a coincidence to be believed.

What was he doing here when he lived in Sicily?

How did he just happen to come to Serifos at the same time as Sam, let alone trail her into some obscure shop?

The more she thought about it, the more his sudden appearance in Greece only days after her arrival here defied logic.

To her knowledge, he'd never tried to find her or her mother. So why now?

The only thing she could think of was that someone had told him she was here, and knew they were father and daughter. But who would do that? No one knew about her connection to Jules Gregory. Except Perseus.

Her heartbeat accelerated to a sickening speed.

Surely *he* wouldn't have contacted her father when he knew she wanted *nothing* to do with her biological parent…

Such a betrayal would mean Perseus had chosen to get involved in something that was none of his business.

He may have bought the painting of her mother from Jules Gregory many years ago. But human decency forbade him to take it a step further, and try to unite her with the man who'd ignored her existence from birth.

If Perseus had done such a thing—and in all likelihood he had, since there could be no other explanation—Sam thought she understood his motives. He'd spent the last twenty years looking for Sofia, and assumed Sam had been on the same quest for her parent.

But Perseus had gone about it behind her back, without her permission. In so doing, he'd committed the unpardonable.

Only someone of Perseus's fame and means, plus his connection through the painting, could cause Jules Gregory to drop whatever he was doing in Sicily, and condescend to show up announcing his paternity after a twenty-four-year silence. Certainly her mother had never been able to affect such a miracle.

The more she thought about it, the more Sam wondered how much money had changed hands to bring about this amazing chance meeting on the streets of the very island where Perseus and her father had done business once before...

What had Perseus offered her father to come all this way to fake a chance meeting with the daughter he'd spawned?

Had her biological parent been promised a gallery of his own in every major city across Europe and the States? How about unlimited funds stashed in a bank account with his name on it, accruing interest in case of a rainy day? Artists occasionally had them... Even a reputed portrait painter like Jules Gregory.

It seemed Perseus had accomplished what anyone else would have deemed the impossible. But in so doing, he'd shattered her last remaining illusions and had caused her world to come crashing down on her head.

With a pain too deep for tears, she turned around to take one last look at the man who was half responsible for getting her into this miserable situation in the first place.

"I'm sorry, sir, but my mother taught me never to speak to strangers."

In the next instant she was behind the wheel of her car. He stood there grim-faced as she backed out. To his credit, he didn't try to detain her as she took off down the street, her tires screeching against the cobblestones.

She'd give him one point for that infinitesimal display of humanity...

Throughout the drive back to the villa, she was scarcely cognizant of the passing scenery. Oddly enough, a great calm had descended. She'd been in such agony wondering how to get through the next eleven months living in the same house with Perseus, not being able to love him. Now her agony was over.

He'd broken a great deal more than his part of their contract. In turn, she was about to break the rest of hers. Since she'd already fulfilled the major part, she felt no shame, no dishonor.

She was leaving Greece, but first she needed her passport and had a hunch it was locked up in his safe in Athens. When she flew there tonight, she'd confront him and get it back. If he dared refuse her, then she'd threaten to tell Sofia everything. In case that threat didn't work, she'd inform him that it was already too late. That she'd left a message for Sofia to be delivered by Yanni no later than ten tonight.

Sam could count on Sofia. As soon as she found out Sam had been hired as his temporary wife to provide a convenient smokescreen until her mourning period had ended, Sofia would do whatever it took to help Sam get her passport back. Sam's plan was foolproof.

One thing she'd learned about Perseus after living with him almost a month. He never operated without a backup plan.

Neither did she. Not anymore.

CHAPTER NINE

TEN minutes later she'd arrived at the villa. The workmen had gone home. It appeared that all the sod had been laid, and the beds stood in readiness for planting.

That would be Sofia's job from here on out.

A sharp, jabbing pain in her heart made Sam jerk her head away. She dashed inside the house.

"Kyria Kostopoulos—"

She eyed the housekeeper, knowing exactly what was coming.

"Your father came by the villa looking for you. I gave him your itinerary. He said that if he couldn't find you, you were to call him at this number."

So the housekeeper was in on Perseus's plan, as well.

The older woman handed her the message on a yellow piece of paper, the kind which had turned Sam's life into a living hell in the first place.

Her initial instincts hadn't been wrong after all... During the descent in Perseus's private elevator at his building in New York, Sam had felt like the prisoner of Hades, the god of the underworld who'd spirited off his prey to his kingdom where a mere mortal would never see the light of day again.

How prophetic.

Too bad Sam hadn't acted on that instinct. It would have saved Perseus a lot of money, and spared her a lifetime of unnecessary, indescribable pain.

"He's staying at the Delphi in Livadi."

"I'll take care of it," Sam murmured, almost choking on the bitterness. "Has my husband called?"

"No, *Kyria.*"

For Perseus not to call was totally out of character.

Sam smirked. *But that was because Perseus had laid a trap and was sitting back to watch.*

"Yanni says to tell you he will be ready to take you to the helicopter at six-thirty."

"Excellent. I'll be ready. And Ariadne, if the phone rings, I'll get it." *Two could play at his game.* "Why don't you and Maria take the rest of the night off? My husband and I will be having dinner in Athens and won't be back until tomorrow evening."

A broad smile broke out on her dark, olive-skinned face. "*Efcharisto, Kyria.*" She gave a slight curtsy before disappearing.

The first thing on Sam's agenda was to go to the study and get a letter written to Sofia. When that was accomplished, she'd take a shower, wash her hair and get dressed to the max. She didn't want to alert Perseus that anything was wrong. Not until she was ready to act.

She'd take two things to Athens; her purse containing seven hundred dollars in *drachma, all Perseus's doing*, which would purchase her a ticket home. An overnight bag with toiletries, a change of underwear, nightware and the same clothes she was wearing, packed inside. She'd leave everything else behind because nothing at the villa belonged to her.

What little she owned—to show she'd taken up space on the planet—had been left in storage in New York. That's where her life had begun. That's where it would end.

With all her plans in place, Sam got to work with a vengeance. Before she knew it, Yanni had brought the car around and they were on their way to Livadi.

"Yanni?" She turned to him. "My husband left this letter to Sofia Leonidas on top of his desk. He wanted her to have it, but he must have gone off without it. When I get to Athens, I'll ask him if he wants it hand-delivered to her. If you haven't heard from either of us by ten o'clock tonight, then will you take it to her, please?''

"*Ne*," he said, yes, tucking it inside his shirt pocket. *So far*, so good.

But the helicopter ride to Athens was something else again. Sam didn't exactly like the sensation which left her stomach floating somewhere outside her body. She decided she preferred the motion of a 747.

When the grinning pilot brought them in for a landing on top of Perseus's office building, she closed her eyes, unable to watch the ground come rushing up to meet them.

"Darling—" She heard Perseus call to her before he lifted her away from the helicopter. "I've been waiting for you."

How did he affect that husky throbbing in his voice? He had to be the greatest actor alive. He could even make his eyes glow with barely concealed passion before his mouth descended.

The pilot could be forgiven for thinking they were madly in love, anxious to find a private place where they could go to give full expression to their love.

Even Sam was shocked by the depth of Perseus's ardor. When she would have pulled away, he demanded more of her, almost devouring her in the process. If he didn't stop, she was going to do the unthinkable and give in to the desire eating her alive. Last night she'd played with fire by allowing herself to fall under his spell. Everything had been a prelude to what was happening right now.

Though her mind and heart knew him to be a traitor, her body didn't seem to understand anything except that it was starving for the kind of assuagement only he could give.

That's when she came to her senses and eased herself

away from him before he was ready. Whispering in his ear she explained, "I-I'm sorry, but I need to use the powder room. The helicopter—"

"Say no more," he murmured back, his voice alive with humor. With another hard kiss to her swollen lips, he cupped her elbow and helped her down the steps. They passed through a security door and entered a corridor. "My suite is right down this hall. The ladies' room is through there."

She muttered a thank-you and headed for the door she could see on her left. The minute she was alone, she slumped against it out of breath.

When she was apart from him, she could think. But in his arms just now, she knew she was in danger of losing her self-respect, her identity, her pride...

No one should allow another person to have that kind of power over them. The charade had to come to an end. She had to finish it *now*.

After a few calming breaths and a repair to her lipstick, she left the powder room and proceeded down the hall where she found him talking to his pilot. Apparently he was giving the other man instructions because every so often the pilot nodded his head.

Perseus looked up when he saw her, his slumberous eyes narrowing on her face and figure. He could stop the acting now. The pilot had gone back up on the roof of the building.

"Would you like a tour of my office before we go to dinner?"

If she didn't know better, she would have accused him of reading her mind. When she thought about it, the building was much smaller and older than the one in New York.

With a nod of her head she said, "Yes. I'd particularly like to see your safe."

His handsome head reared back and he burst out

laughing. Evidently she'd said something totally unexpected. "Since it seems to matter to you so much, I'd even let you see inside it, *if* I had one."

Her eyes widened in alarm. "You mean you don't?"

"No. Anything of real value I keep in a safe-deposit box at the bank."

Crushed by the news, she turned her head aside, pretending interest in the furnishings which were done in classic Greek style. It was Saturday night. "Can you get into your safe-deposit box on the weekend?"

He took a step closer to her, obviously intrigued. "Of course. Why this burning interest? Do you have something valuable you wish me to lock up for you?"

Damn him for behaving as if he didn't know what had happened to her today. His meddling had brought her face-to-face with her own father!

She took a deep breath. "More to the point, Perseus, I'd like you to get something out for me."

One dark brow quirked. "You must know something about the contents that I don't. You're being very cryptic tonight, Kyria Kostopoulos."

Hardening her resolve she retorted, "And you're being your usual invincible, godlike self. Your attractive mask is in place. I don't even see a betraying twitch along that masterful jaw to tell me that you're capable of human error like the rest of us foolish mortals who try to mind our own business and keep out of harm's way."

He didn't move. He didn't say anything. But in an instant, something colder and harder than the marble beneath their feet shot through his powerful body, altering him drastically.

"Your innuendoes have found their mark," came the grating voice. His withering gaze centered on her, shriveling her up emotionally. "Are you going to enlighten me why I'm suddenly damned in your eyes?" he asked with deadly calm. "Or do you expect me to guess what has happened to turn your tongue into a lethal weapon."

Hot spots stained her cheeks crimson. "Play all the boardroom games you want with anyone else, but not with me! You already know what I'm alluding to, so there's no point in talking about it. I'd like my passport back."

His eyes studied her taut features for endless moments. "You thought I kept it in my safe…"

"Or your deposit box. Whatever."

Another tension-filled pause stretched between them. "Are you planning a trip somewhere?"

"Not a trip. I'm going back to New York."

"To visit old friends?" he baited in that silky tone guaranteed to raise her blood pressure.

"To live out the rest of my life!" The sharpness of her declaration reverberated in the enclosed suite.

"You're perfectly free to do that in a little less than a year's time."

She flashed him a contemptuous smile. "That's right. We struck a bargain. But you did something that nullifies our contract, and now I want out of it."

His hands went to his hips, drawing her attention to the coffee colored silk suit he was wearing for their evening out. The cloth revealed rock-hard thigh muscles. His stunning jacket molded to the breadth of his shoulders. When he moved, the sound of the silk whispered of unleashed power and sinew beneath the elegant material.

"If you had asked—" He slanted her an unfathomable glance. "I would have told you that your passport is in the top right-hand drawer of my desk on Serifos."

Her spirits plummeted. She'd thought of peeking in his desk, but at the last second her conscience hadn't allowed it.

"Frankly, I'm surprised you didn't find it and escape without my knowledge."

"No. That's something *you* would do," she threw back at him, causing his brows to furrow into an uncompromising black line. "I've tried to do the honorable thing by coming to you and asking to be released from our contract."

His eyes were shuttered as he murmured, "If the infraction I supposedly committed were truly as earth-shaking as you've made it out to be, I might be persuaded to let you go...provided you tell me the reason for your outrage."

"Cruelty appears to be one of your less enviable traits after all, but I suppose no man could rise to your heights without stooping to that level from time to time."

"Be careful what you say *Kyria*," he warned, clearly at the edge of his patience.

That worked both ways.

"Or what?" she goaded, her eyes exploding blue flame. "Will you repeat history and have me locked up in a Turkish convent? Is there no man on earth a woman can trust?"

A frightening stream of Greek invective poured out of him. She unconsciously started backing away. He was so livid she must have imagined the brief glint of pain she thought she saw in his eyes before they became veiled.

"No one talks to me that way, not even *you*."

"I just did. If you want an explanation, it's all there in the letter to Sofia."

His face darkened with lines. "What letter?" he demanded savagely.

"The one Yanni has been instructed to deliver to her personally if I haven't recovered my passport by ten tonight."

Maybe it was true that the hand was quicker than the

eye. She couldn't have had time to blink before he pulled out his cellular phone and was pushing numbers.

She swallowed hard when she realized that Perseus's forbidding black gaze was daring her to make one move toward the door of his suite. She had the strongest suspicion that no one had ever defied him to this extreme and lived to get away with it.

He held his hand over the mouthpiece. "It's ten past nine. Do I ask Yanni to open the letter and read it to me, thereby exposing all our lives to the gossip mongers and causing Sofia more grief?" he asked in lethal tones, "or do *you* want to do the honors? I'm giving you a choice. Something you didn't give me." His words dropped like a shrouded corpse delivered into the deep.

Sam groaned when she thought of the damage that letter could do if it got into the hands of the press. After a few seconds, "I thought my plan was infallible, but I should have remembered I'm playing against one of the world's recognized geniuses in the take-over department."

She hated the triumphant gleam that entered those black depths. "I take it that you've decided to cooperate," he came back smoothly, sounding completely unruffled. Her insult hadn't made a dent in that godlike armor.

"T-tell Yanni I made a mistake, and ask him not to mail it."

Perseus rapped out something in his native tongue, then put the phone back in his jacket pocket. With arms folded, he lounged negligently against the front of his desk. "I'm waiting for an explanation, *Kyria*."

He used that endearment to undermine her, but she wasn't about to fall for it again.

"Do you deny that you wanted to unite me with my father?"

"No," he said with such honesty and speed, she couldn't think for a moment.

"Even when I told you that I never wanted to talk or think about him again?" By now her entire body was trembling.

"Even then," he answered boldly. "Sometimes things aren't what they seem, as we both found out where Sofia was concerned."

Tears filled her eyes. *Damn*.

"Don't you dare compare Sofia's experience to mine. I had a mother who told me everything I'd ever need to know about my biological father."

A troubled look entered his eyes. "Sometimes a parent sees the truth they want to see."

Her chin lifted. "My mother's truth *was* the truth."

He straightened to his full height, leveling his penetrating gaze fully on her. "Are you absolutely certain about that? I believed in my mother implicitly. But it doesn't change the fact that she never told me Sofia's father had always carried a torch for her, let alone that he'd asked her to marry him before she accepted my own father's proposal."

His face darkened with lines. "That sin of omission caused me untold grief because I never understood my stepfather's resentment of me. In the end, it changed my destiny and Sofia's."

Try as she would, she couldn't discount his logic entirely. The pain was starting again, even greater than before. "Unfortunately my mother isn't alive to question." Her voice shook.

"That's right," he inserted strongly. "But someone else is. In fact he's the only person who can put all the missing pieces together."

"*No*—" Sam cried out in anguish. "Don't you understand anything? You, who the other night told me that unless a gift was given freely, then you wanted no part of it?''

''I said that,'' came his maddening admission.

To her shame, her face glistened with tears. ''If my father had wanted me in his life, then I wouldn't have had to endure the unwanted attention of a total stranger twenty-four years later, and ask him, 'Do I know you?' before he announced his name was Jules Gregory, *my beloved father*!''

She would have fought Perseus, but her pain was too great. The second she felt those powerful arms enfold her, she began sobbing. Deep, wrenching sobs. The shock of seeing her flesh-and-blood parent for the first time was only now catching up with her.

''Did he come to the villa?'' he whispered, sounding oddly anxious.

''No. He followed me from the apothecary in Livadi.'' She struggled to get the words out. ''Why did you do it, Perseus? Why did you find him and make him come? I've never needed him. All these years he's been dead to me. Didn't you realize what it would do to me to see him in person?'' she cried angrily, and pushed herself away from him.

For once Perseus didn't pursue her. He stayed where he was, his expression solemn.

''If that's the way you really feel, *Kyria*, then I'll take steps to make sure he never bothers you again.''

She lifted her tear-stained face to his piercing gaze. ''If you mean that, then you'll let me leave for New York tonight.''

A certain stillness crept over him. ''I'll release you from our contract on two conditions.''

''No!'' She shook her head, causing her hair to swish. ''I won't face my father one more time, not even for you,'' she said before she realized what she'd given away. Now he knew how deeply her emotions were involved where he was concerned. It was too much!

"This has nothing to do with your father. This has to do with *me*."

She buried her face in her hands. "What are you talking about?"

"Tonight I had intended to take you out for some Greek dancing. But I think we'll forego that pleasure and simply enjoy the surprise I had planned for you afterward."

"Surprise?" She mouthed the word, scarcely coherent.

"Yes. I had my sailboat stocked with provisions so we could enjoy a night crossing. You haven't been to the other islands yet. Tomorrow I thought we'd stop at several on our way back to Serifos."

Under any other circumstances it would have sounded like heaven. A groan escaped her lips unbidden.

"If you're amenable, we'll follow through with my plan. Once we arrive on Serifos, I'll give you your passport and you can take the helicopter back to Athens for your flight home."

He was being too reasonable. "What's the other condition?" she asked in a dull voice, her heart breaking.

"That you live with me as my wife in New York until the waiting period is over. The same stipulations of our agreement will apply. I'll establish you in the New York plant. You'll have the freedom to see your friends and do the things you've been missing. Most important of all, you'll have put five thousand miles of ocean between you and your father."

At that comment, her head lifted.

No matter how angry she was with the way he'd interfered in a matter that was none of his concern, she couldn't doubt his sincerity. The fact that he'd answered her questions honestly and forthrightly proved that much at least.

If *she* were honest, she would admit that somewhere inside she loved him even more for trying to get her and her father together. But since his plan had failed, he was trying to do everything in his power to make amends.

Living in New York with its hundreds of distractions wouldn't be nearly as impossible as living with him on Serifos. And there was another truth she had to admit to herself. She couldn't bear the thought of Perseus accidentally bumping into Sofia all the time in Sam's presence.

No. If she stayed with him, then residing in the States was the only solution that made any sense. The fact remained that their initial contract was still in force. She *had* agreed to live with him for propriety's sake until he could marry Sofia. If she went along with this new contract, she could honor her commitment to him and still make a life for herself.

At least in New York she could stay busy with her old friends and try to recapture the life she'd once led before a man named Perseus put a tentacle hold on her heart.

The trouble was, no man could ever measure up to him. He was the stuff myths were made of, which was why she needed to get back to reality, as soon as possible.

It felt a little like *déjà vu* when she filled her lungs with air and said, "I accept your conditions."

His face was an inscrutable mask. "Be very sure. I won't allow you to go back on your word this time."

"I'm sure," came her empathic answer, formulating a new plan of her own.

Since she knew she'd never find another man like him, she could at least make a real career for herself. It would mean working night and day, exactly what she needed to try and exorcize him from her consciousness.

"So be it," he murmured in a satisfied tone. "Now that we have business out of the way, I've discovered I'm hungry." He pulled out his cellular phone, most likely alerting his pilot that they were ready to go.

"The sooner we take off for Pireaus, the sooner we can be at sea. Tonight the thought of sharing a meal with only the moon and stars for an audience, holds great appeal."

Nothing sounded more romantic. But Sam couldn't get the picture of Perseus and Sofia out of her mind. They'd once sailed to Delos to pledge their love to each other. Children of the sea, the Greeks.

Unlike the voyage of the mythical god Perseus however, her own real-live Perseus was returning home to Serifos chained to the wrong woman. How bittersweet this must be for him. He'd conquered the world, yet his own adored, black-haired Andromeda was still unavailable to him.

Right then Sam could have wept for him, for herself. For the unfairness of life which held true fulfillment out of reach. She'd come achingly close to finding it with Perseus, only to discover that it was a foolish dream. Like all dreams spun by mere mortals, it had to end when the first light of day caused it to evaporate as if it had never been...

CHAPTER TEN

No MATTER how hard Sam tried to deny it, she felt a poignant sense of homecoming as Perseus sailed with an expertise learned almost from birth, into the harbor at Livadi beneath a blazing, late-afternoon sun.

The mystic isles of Kythnos, Sifnos and Milos were already an enchanting memory only Perseus with his intimate knowledge of their secrets could have made possible. More bittersweet memories to take back to New York...

Dressed in the same outfit she'd worn to town the day before, Sam alighted from the immaculate interior to help tie the ropes to the dock. Under Perseus's careful tutelege, she was learning fast and had already gained her sea legs. In her heart of hearts, she wished they could have sailed on indefinitely.

As he was securing the boat, he suddenly flashed her a carefree smile. With his black hair attractively disheveled, his skin bronzed by the elements, he looked ten years younger. She felt the staggering pain of love pierce her very soul.

Though she'd never had a desire to draw humans before, she found herself needing to capture this picture of him on canvas. Before the day was out, she'd make an initial sketch. It would be her greatest treasure.

"Kyria Kostopoulos—" He broke in on her reverie, his voice sounding amazingly happy for a man with a permanent heartache. "You've made your husband proud today. Now you deserve a rest. While I gather up the luggage and see to a few details, you go on ahead. Yanni will be waiting for us at the end of the pier."

Was Perseus tired of her? Now that they'd arrived on Serifos, was the knowledge that Sofia lived close by the reason he wanted some time to himself?

"You mean you're not going to make me swab the deck?" she teased to cover her pain, hating the idea of being separated from him, even for a second.

"That will be lesson number two," he came back in the same playful mood.

She fought to keep her smile in place. Given her freedom when she wanted it least, she had no choice but to do as he suggested, knowing full well there would *never* be a second lesson.

Conquering the urge to look back one last time, she made her way along the floating dock, aware that such intense joy as she'd just experienced was ephemeral. Away from him, it had gone out of the day, depriving her of the ability to marvel over the picturesque setting.

As she dodged the local foot traffic coming and going along the pier, she was scarcely cognizant of the myriad of boats—all different sizes and types—moored inside the sheltered bay.

"*Signomi*," she excused herself when she almost bumped into someone who'd unexpectedly stepped into her path.

"Samantha?"

She gasped at the sound of the familiar voice and looked around. Once again she found herself face-to-face with her father.

Another chance meeting Perseus had engineered? All it would have taken was a call from his cellular phone. "I'll produce your daughter at the dock by five o'clock. The rest is up to you."

She didn't think she could feel any more pain over Perseus's betrayal, but she was wrong. Gone was all desire to capture his memory on paper.

While she was attempting to fight herself out of the

emotional maelstrom in which she'd been flung, her father had been taking private inventory of her face and hair.

Yesterday they'd both been wearing sunglasses. Today, they were minus their disguises. Though she was loathe to admit it, he was an extremely handsome man in his own right. The one tiny photo she'd ever seen of him came from a magazine article. He'd been wearing sunglasses and a hat, making it impossible for her to get a clear picture of his features.

Despite all the emotions boiling up inside of her, she found it fascinating that his eyes were the same shape, the same intense blue as her own. That their mouths followed identical lines and curves, that their hair grew from the same side part. Genetic links offering indisputable proof of their father-daughter connection.

"I'm sorry Perseus's misguided sense of family forced you to come all the way from Sicily for nothing. I've gotten along just fine all these years without a father, and don't need one now." For once her voice didn't betray her with a stupid wobble or some such humiliating thing.

There was a slight pause, then, "Don't blame your husband for my appearance," he began quietly. "The truth is, I've gotten along fine without a daughter all these years, as well. That is, until I saw a picture of you and your illustrious spouse in a local Sicilian newspaper. When he was a younger man, he bought my painting of your mother."

She nodded soberly. "I know."

He pursed his lips. "The article said you were the former Samantha Telford, that you'd been recently married in New York, and had come home to your new villa on Serifos."

His steady gaze shone with too much compassion for her liking. "Telford was your grandfather's last name.

But even if your name hadn't seemed to be too much of a coincidence, I knew that genes don't lie. I studied your picture for hours, haunted by the uncanny resemblance to your mother.'' His voice shook.

''Anna—a woman who has come to mean a great deal to me—agreed there was a true mystery here. She insisted that I come. You see... I was terrified that if I discovered you really were my flesh and blood, that you'd hate the very sight of me. I wasn't sure I could handle that.

''But after several days, it became clear to me that I'd never find peace until I came to Serifos and met you in person. Your housekeeper told me where I might find you.'' He inhaled sharply. ''One look at you yesterday and I knew you were my daughter.'' The last came out in a husky tone.

Sam couldn't take it in. Perseus had not been involved in their meeting after all. An enormous weight seemed to lift from her heart, only to be replaced by remorse because she'd falsely accused him.

''I—I'm sorry I was so horrible to you yesterday.''

''It was entirely understandable, but I was prepared to take any risk to find out if I really did have a child.''

Again, she reeled because her father had come looking for her without any help from Perseus. And Perseus had let her heap abuse on his head without saying a word to defend himself. *What had she done*?

''I never stopped loving your mother, even though she refused to marry me, never answered my phone calls or my letters after I left Cheyenne.''

Cheyenne? Her father had been to Cheyenne? When?

''But I'm not sure I will ever be able to forgive her for keeping your existence a secret from me.''

A secret—

She could hardly breathe. *Was Perseus right*? Was her mother's truth only *part* of the whole *truth*?

"Y-you really didn't know about me?"

"No."

She heard a whole world of meaning in that one word. It came to her then. *He couldn't possibly be lying.*

"One thing I will say in her defense." His eyes glinted with unshed tears. "Between the two of us, we created a genuine masterpiece."

Sam bit her lip, overwhelmed by the compliment he'd just paid her. "Thank you," she finally whispered, her emotions in chaos.

Then a pained expression crossed his face. "How is your mother?"

Sam could hardly swallow. "She died last year."

A bleakness entered her father's eyes. Whatever had gone wrong between her parents, it was obvious he had suffered.

"Why don't we get out of the heat and go back to the villa to talk?" Perseus spoke up before she could form the rest of her thoughts.

The two men acknowledged each other and shook hands. "It's been a long time, Mr. Gregory."

"Call me, Jules."

Sam had no idea how long Perseus had been standing there listening, but she was grateful when she felt his hands slide to her shoulders from behind in a warm, firm grip. It was as if he knew she was emotionally overwrought and would collapse any second without support.

Her father's gaze left Perseus to fall upon her once more. There was a pronounced pallor to his skin as he quietly asked, "Is that what *you* want, Samantha? If not, I'll go away and never bother you again."

"No!" The spontaneous cry leaped from her throat. "I need to know why mother did what she did, why she sent you away. I want to get to know my father.

"For years I hated you because I thought you didn't want me. I learned that you were living in Sicily, and I told myself I didn't care. But I realize that my hate was just a defense to prevent me from looking for you. The fear that you'd reject me was too great. Please— Don't go," she begged.

"Thank God you said that."

She watched her father stand there and weep. It was too much. When he held out his arms, she didn't hesitate to move into them.

"It's incredible," he murmured. "I have a little girl, only she's a beautiful, grown woman."

Sam couldn't talk. She was too dissolved in tears.

"Do you have a car, Jules?"

He had to clear his throat several times before addressing Perseus. "Yes. I rented one. It's at the Athenian where I'm staying." He looked down at Sam. "Much as I hate letting you out of my sight, it might be better if you go home with your husband. I'll meet you there after I've had a shower. I've been waiting for you all day, and need to freshen up."

"All day?"

His smile was one of her father's most attractive traits. "Your housekeeper said you were out sailing today, but she had no idea when you would return to port. I wasn't about to take any chances on missing you."

Sam wiped her eyes with her palms. "If you hadn't seen that picture in the newspaper, we might never have met."

"I don't even want to think about it," her father said rather emotionally, then gave her another hug before he let her go and swiftly turned to leave.

"Don't take too long," Sam cried out.

Her father waved before breaking into a run.

Perseus stood a little ways apart from Sam, eyeing her through hooded eyes. "Your father was trying to do the right thing when he suggested that you come back to the villa with me. But I saw the way he was looking at you.

If you'd rather join him at the hotel for a private reunion, I have no doubts he'd be overjoyed.''

"He acted happy, didn't he?" Her voice came out more like a croak.

"That's the understatement of all time," he drawled.

She flushed. "Still— I think he needs a little time to assimilate everything.''

"And you?"

"I-I've always known he was alive. Twenty-four years has given me a lot of lead time, whereas h-he has only known he had a daughter since yesterday." She lowered her head. "Perseus— Forgive me for accusing you of trying to manipulate my life. I said awful things to you last night.''

He picked up their bags and urged her forward. "Don't ask my forgiveness, Samantha. A few more weeks and you would have had every right to be furious with me, so we won't speak of it again.''

Her head jerked around. "You mean you were going to try to find him?"

"Yes." Again, his blunt honesty caught her off guard.

They walked to the car where Yanni stood waiting. While Perseus stowed their bags in the trunk, she asked Yanni for the letter she'd given him.

Once she and Perseus were ensconced in the back seat, Yanni started the car and they were off.

She felt her husband's eyes on the letter in her hands. "It seems we're both still capable of surprising each other.''

A wave of heat enveloped her body. "I wasn't quite in my right mind when I wrote this. Here." She held it out to him.

He shook his head. "I know how you think, and I understand your motives. Throw it away, Samantha.''

She crumpled it up in her palm. "I shouldn't have questioned yours," she whispered in a shaky voice.

"But you did. In fact you're still bristling with resentment. All right, *Kyria*. To satisfy your curiosity—when we were in your apartment and I told you I would grant you three wishes, your behavior led me to believe there was a fourth wish, one you refused to voice aloud.

"After you saw the painting in my bedroom, and I witnessed the depth of your pain where your father is concerned, it came as a revelation that his absence from your life has always held the key to your rather complicated psyche."

Perseus understood her better than she did herself.

"I had to wait twenty years for answers which I badly needed, and thought if I could spare you even one more day of wasted energy in that department, I would."

A heavy sigh escaped her lips, another regret because she'd doubted him.

"Thank you for explaining. The truth is, initially I might have been angry with you, but I would have gotten over it. Meeting my father...realizing that this has all come as a shock to him... Well—it puts an entirely different complexion on everything."

A strong, suntanned hand reached out and covered hers. "One of your sterling qualities is your generous heart, *Kyria*."

"But I should have had more trust," she blurted, not ready to forgive herself.

He squeezed her hand gently. "The important thing is that you found out you are wanted and loved. No human can ask for more than that."

The huskiness in his voice betrayed him, plunging her into a deeper abyss. Perseus was referring to Sofia as well as her own father. Just thinking of the other woman, let alone imagining her in Perseus's arms, was unbearable. Sam didn't know she was capable of this kind of jealousy, an emotion unworthy of her, but she couldn't seem to help it.

Wanting to make absolution for her wretched thoughts she ventured, "If you'd like, we could have a small dinner party before we leave for New York."

Clearly she'd surprised him. "You want to do this to honor your father?"

"Actually, I was thinking of you and Sofia," she said in a quiet voice so Yanni couldn't hear. "It must be agony for you to be contemplating our move to New York. If she were seen at the villa in the company of a few close friends, no one would think anything about it. At some point in the evening, you could find yourselves alone a-and say your goodbyes in private.

"I'm sure eleven months' separation is going to feel like an eternity to both of you." The last came out a little jerkily. How she hated it when she lost control of her voice.

His love for Sofia was so great, he probably didn't realize he was crushing her hand in reaction. "Again, your generosity astounds me," he murmured, sounding so remote she knew he was imagining himself on their private beach, covering Sofia's body with his own.

She stared out the window, but couldn't stop those pictures from filling her mind. Perseus must have been having the same trouble because he suddenly let go of her hand, as if he couldn't bear anyone's touch but Sofia's.

Bereft of his emotional and physical comfort, Sam was counting the minutes until she could reach the privacy of her own room and give in to the feelings swamping her.

Being reunited with her father had contributed a huge amount to her highly emotional state. But she couldn't lie to herself any longer. Knowing that Perseus would never love her, make love to her, was the most catastrophic thing that had ever happened to her.

She could see nothing in her future but a devastating

emptiness. There was only one Perseus Kostopoulos. She could search to and fro, over the face of the whole earth, and never find his equal. No other man could even come close.

Whom did she think she was kidding when she'd told herself she could get on with her old life once they'd returned to New York. What a joke!

What an absurd joke.

Then another devastating thought inserted itself. It was entirely possible Perseus knew how she felt about him. Dear God.

She and Perseus had never slept together, never consummated their marriage, though on several occasions they'd come close. But it had always been Perseus who pulled away first, *because he knew that an annulment would ensure that he could turn right around and marry Sofia the next day.*

A divorce could take months beyond Sofia's period of mourning, a risk Perseus had no desire to take after waiting so long…

Because he was such a decent man, that was probably the real reason he'd intended on trying to get her and her father together. Who better to cling to? Who better to help her heal from the loss after he let her go for good?

But in that assumption Perseus was wrong!

Whatever the future held in store for her and father, he'd been leading his own life for close to sixty years. Obviously this woman, Anna, was the love in his life now. Things weren't going to change because he'd discovered that he had a daughter. Except that she was hoping they would develop a close relationship over the coming years.

But nothing, or no one, could repair the damage from losing Perseus. He filled more than a hole in her heart. He had possession of the whole thing.

Somehow her career was going to have to be the miracle cure for helping her deal with her grief. Perseus had said she could get started on it as soon as they reached New York. If she—

"Samantha?"

She whipped her head around, wondering how long he'd been trying to get her attention.

"Yes?" she answered tentatively.

"You're concern over Sofia's and my feelings is laudable. But I'm afraid that giving a dinner party on the pretext of throwing the two of us together is out of the question."

"Because a person in mourning isn't allowed to go out?" Sam couldn't imagine such an absurd custom.

"No, *Kyria*. Sofia left unfinished business in Turkey. She's returning there tomorrow."

How did he know that? Had he been on the phone with her?

Her hand tortured the armrest. *Sam—you've got to stop this. What he does out of your sight is none of your business.*

"H-how long will she be gone, do you think?"

"I presume for as long as it takes."

The remoteness of his tone made Sam shudder. He had to be going through another hell right now, knowing she'd be leaving Greece tomorrow.

Her thoughts were working fast and furiously. She doubted Yanni could follow any of their conversation, being separated as they were in the car, plus the fact that he only knew the basic rudiments of English. But to make sure, she turned and nestled closer to Perseus, as if she were about to kiss him.

"Perseus—" she whispered near his ear, "when we get home, why don't you give all the help the night off. Everybody. Then I'll go for Sofia and bring her back to the villa with me. Surely there'd be nothing wrong with two women being together. My father and I could go out on the beach for our talk, leaving you and Sofia alone for a while. It isn't fair that she go away again withou—"

"What you're suggesting is impossible." He cut her off, his chest heaving from the force of his emotions held barely in check. "Does this self-sacrificing streak of yours have limits, *Kyria*? Or do I dare wish that you would offer me *your* arms for the solace I seek, but cannot find," he ground out.

By the time she'd digested what he'd just said, his mouth had captured hers with smothering force, demanding a response she would have given him because she couldn't help herself, *if* she hadn't known he was taking out his frustrations on her.

Perseus began kissing her with a depth of passion she had no idea existed. But a little voice inside cried that this passion existed for another woman, not Sam.

Talking about Sofia had been exactly the wrong thing to do. Because she'd meddled in his personal life and had attempted to get the two of them together, Sam had fueled the fire of his suppressed longing for the woman he loved above all else.

Yanni could be forgiven for thinking Perseus couldn't wait to get home to make love to his wife. But Sam knew this total ravishment of her senses was a form of punishment because Perseus held the wrong woman in his arms. She'd unwittingly aroused the sleeping tiger, and now she must pay the price.

But it was a divine price...

Every kiss grew deeper until she couldn't remember ever doing anything else. Drugged by the sensations his hands and mouth created, she could feel herself slipping into that dangerous zone of sensual pleasure where there was no right or wrong. Only need remained, a powerful need that forgot honor or propriety.

"*Perseus*—" she gasped when his mouth left hers to kiss her throat where the scent of her perfume lingered. "What will Yanni think?" Her voice came out slurred.

"Exactly what I want him to think," he whispered against her velvet skin, defeating her little moan of protest.

"But we're home." She was fighting his lips in earnest now. "My father will be arriving at any moment."

"All he'll think is that we're happily married, and desperately in love."

"But we're not!" With a tiny cry she pushed her palms against the solid wall of his chest.

Maybe she'd gotten through to him because his hands finally slid down her arms and fell away. "I refuse to give my father the wrong impression. He needs to know why we married in the first place, so he won't be shocked when we're no longer together next summer."

On that note of finality, she dashed from the car and into the house before she broke down and confessed her guilty secret, that she'd fallen irrevocably in love with him.

While she slipped out of her clothes and showered, she relived those moments in his arms. When she emerged minutes later to brush her hair till it gleamed, her body was still on fire from his touch. Tonight he'd transported her to a point where there would have been no turning back if she'd allowed the insanity to continue another second.

It was insanity, on both their parts. His, because his pain over Sofia's imminent departure had become so excruciating. Hers, because she hadn't taken steps to prevent this kind of thing from happening.

It was her fault. Every bit of it. She'd asked Yanni for the letter back instead of waiting until she could find him alone. That letter had sent Perseus over the edge. When she'd brushed up against him to suggest she bring

Sofia to the house, Perseus had retaliated, totally unaware of her love for him.

Well…there'd be no repeat performance of that shatteringly sensual experience, she chastised herself furiously as she slipped into a periwinkle-blue cotton sundress with spaghetti straps.

In the morning they were leaving for New York and a new life which she planned would be so filled with purpose and hectic, she and Perseus would rarely see each other, let alone find time for anything to happen of such an earthshaking nature as tonight's episode in the car.

While she was putting on her white sandals she heard a knock on the door. Sam's heartbeat tripled because she thought it was Perseus. Instead it was Ariadne calling out to inform Sam that her father had arrived and was waiting for her in the salon.

''I'll be right there,'' she answered back, thanking heaven that she had a father who'd come looking for her as soon as he'd known of her existence. Especially now, at this precarious moment in her life when she needed a buffer against Perseus's powerful charisma. It was almost like divine intervention.

The feeling persisted when she rushed into the salon a minute later to be embraced once more by her attractive parent who'd come in a pastel blue suit and paisley tie, something he said he rarely wore, in honor of this occasion which was the happiest moment of his life.

That comment started the tears flowing once more. Though Sam's mother wasn't a toucher by nature, her father more than made up for it. He was obviously a demonstrative man whose emotions ran deep and clamored to find expression through his fabulous paintings.

Perseus hadn't made an appearance yet. Sam had an idea he was purposely giving her and her father a chance to really get acquainted before they ate dinner.

For a few minutes they delighted in making a visual exploration of each other, picking out all the physical similarities that announced their blood bond. Soon their conversation turned to those behavioral traits they had in common, like the way they cocked their head to the left side, the broadness of their smiles, their discomfiture with large crowds, their reticence to share their problems with others, their need to be alone when they worked out a problem.

"You two have a great deal more in common than that," a deep masculine voice suddenly interjected.

How long had Perseus been standing there listening while they were engrossed in conversation on the long, white sectional couch near the windows?

Sam's head whirled around. To her shock, he'd brought all of her tablecloths and fabric samples with him. They were draped over his arms.

"When we first met, I found these in Sam's bedroom closet," he announced without shame, uncaring that her father would get the wrong idea completely about her relationship with Perseus before their marriage. "I told her she had a spark of genius in her. What I didn't know then was that she had the blood of Jules Gregory running through her veins."

"Let me see those." Her father got up from the couch and began scrutinizing everything Perseus had laid out over the chairs. She found herself holding her breath. "Honey—your husband's right." He sounded really excited.

"Your work reminds me a little of a Matisse painting, but it's all original, all your own brilliant style. Your use of rich color is nothing short of phenomenal." He turned his dark-blond head to look at her. In a voice full of tears he said, "I'm so proud of you, I feel like I'm going to burst."

"Thank you," she whispered, absolutely positive a

human being couldn't contain this much happiness and not explode, especially after a compliment like that coming from her famous father.

"This is only the tip of the iceberg." Perseus continued to speak to him without a shred of modesty for her.

"She has designed our entire yard and garden. I have no doubts that when all her plans come to fruition, my villa will be a showplace everyone in the Cyclades will stop by to visit. We'll have to charge admission."

At that statement her father burst into hearty laughter and Sam joined him. Perseus was smiling, even with his eyes, a sight she rarely saw.

"Before long," her husband went on undaunted, "she'll be besieged by people wanting her to landscape their yards. However, that's not her latest claim to fame."

Sam stared at him, wondering what he was getting at.

In that low, vibrant voice he added, "Her senior art project took first prize at the university a week ago, and is now hanging in the foyer of my office building in New York. A bronze plaque given by the department stating her name, year and award has been mounted below the frame. There's also a ten thousand dollar check on its way to her."

Her father's cry of delight filled the room, but Perseus's unexpected news had sent her into shock, robbing her of the happiness she'd been feeling.

The mention of money reminded her that he'd given an enormous sum to the art department as part of their bargain. Did her professor have any choice but to award the prize to her?

Perseus watched the blood drain from her face.

"I know what you're thinking." He read her mind with incredible ease. "It's true I've established that fund for deserving artists. All the papers were prepared before we left New York. But I instructed my attorney to hold off contacting the department for an initial conference until the winners of the project were announced first.''

It was a good thing she was sitting down. To be plunged from the depths to the heights in the space of a few seconds had practically immobilized her.

"Perhaps more than you," he muttered soberly, "I wanted you to win that prize on the strength of your superb talent. Nothing else."

"*Perseus*—" she squealed for joy, the sudden rush of adrenaline bringing her to her feet. "You're really not making this up? I won first place?"

"How could you doubt it?"

His mouth curved in one of those miraculous smiles that melted her bones. She felt as if they were the only two people on earth.

"Before you and I left for Greece, I gave your friend, Lois, my office phone number in Athens. I asked her to let me know the results the minute Professor Giddings had made his decision."

"You're kidding!" Sam couldn't take it in. "Lois informed you?"

"That's right. She said to tell you that you still owe her a tablecloth. She thinks it's going to be worth a fortune someday because it's a Samantha Telford original. I happen to agree with her," he supplied smoothly.

"Since I'm the reason why you made her such a rash promise in the first place, I hope you don't mind if I told her you'd make her a gift of it as soon as you were set up in your own business, and had no more use for it as a prototype."

His face grew pensive. "I also hope you aren't too upset that I didn't tell you right away. The simple fact is, I felt a little like Santa Claus and wished it were Christmas so I could put your present under the tree. Barring that, I wanted to choose the right moment."

After a pause, "I'm quite certain that being united

with your father is probably the supreme moment of your life, isn't that so, *Kyria*?''

"Perseus—" her father interjected emotionally, raising his arm to hug his daughter.

Sam knew exactly how her parent felt, but was incapable of speech.

"Two geniuses in one family meeting for the first time warrants a celebration. What could be more timely than the announcement of your prize? A coveted honor from the most celebrated art department in the U.S." Fearing he'd see the love light in her eyes, she hid her face in her father's shoulder.

I love you, Perseus, and it's killing me...

"I'll inform Maria we're ready for dinner. Come out to the patio when you're ready."

Sam was thankful Perseus left the salon when he did. Otherwise he would have seen her break down in her father's arms.

"We may have not known each other very long, honey, but I have a feeling these tears aren't all for joy."

Her father saw too much.

"It's obvious that Perseus Kostopoulos is the great love of your life. It's equally apparent that he feels the same way about you. So what is it that is breaking your heart? I may have missed out on your first twenty-four years, but I'm here now, and plan to be for the duration. Let me shoulder some of the burden. I'm a good listener."

All the parental love and sincerity she could wish for was there in his voice, crumbling the barriers she'd erected over a lifetime.

She found herself blurting the entire story about her and Perseus. "...So you see. It's all an act on his part."

"No," her father refuted with surprising intensity. "Only love motivates a man to do what he did for you tonight."

She shook her head sadly and moved out of his arms. "Perseus is the greatest actor alive."

"You mean like your own mother?"

Sam glanced at him with haunted eyes. She'd been waiting for an opening to find out why her parents had gone their own way.

"What happened?"

He smoothed a strand of hair from her forehead. "Your mother and I fell headlong in love one summer while I was in Cheyenne working on a series of Indian paintings. Those were the early days of my career. I was a poor, struggling artist from the west coast who lived where my painting took me.

"In those days I wasn't marriage material. My finances were nonexistent. I lived hand to mouth. But none of it mattered because my painting was everything.

"At least that's what I told myself until I met your mother. By the end of the summer, I was prepared to get a job in Cheyenne so I could marry her. I'm not saying I would have given up my painting. But I wanted her enough that I was willing to settle down and find a way to do my painting on the side." After a brief silence, "She turned me down, honey."

"I'm so sorry," Sam whispered.

"She told me that she'd had a great time with me, but she wasn't in love with me." He shook his head. "I knew she was lying, so I proposed over and over again. But I couldn't break her down."

"Mother had no self-confidence," Sam admitted sadly.

"You're right. With hindsight I could see that she was afraid of holding me back from my destiny. She always did believe in my ability to paint. But at the time I was in too much pain from her rejection to stay in Cheyenne, so I left for Flathead country in Montana. That was my mistake. I wrote her every day. She never answered one of my letters. I tried phoning her, but she wouldn't talk to me.

"Eventually I went to New York and was lucky enough to sell some of my work. I wrote her again, telling her I'd received my first major commission, that I had enough money for us to get married. I sent her a plane ticket, and prayed for a response. Nothing."

Sam knew how stubborn her mother could be.

"I think at that point I gave up and left for Europe. I reached my lowest ebb here on Serifos where I was doing a series of paintings on the Greek myths. Then fate in the form of your husband stepped in. He hounded me in his inimitable way to sell him that painting of your mother.

"I decided it was time to let her go. From that point on, I never looked back." His eyes blazed with a strange light. "But if I'd had any idea she was carrying my child, I would have returned to Cheyenne and forced her to marry me."

Sam bowed her head. "I believe you. The problem is, she never spoke about the past, but I know now she must have regretted that decision terribly because she was sick most of her life, and died far too young."

"She never married?"

"No. I doubt she ever looked at another man."

He let out a heavy sigh. "The scars run deep. I'm afraid I never considered marriage again, either."

Taking her courage in her hands she asked, "How long have you been with Anna?"

"Eleven years."

A smile curved her lips. "I've heard of men having premarital jitters, but eleven years? Don't you think it's time you popped the question?"

He looked taken back, then he chuckled and gave her another hug.

"I think you have a point."

"Dad—" Her voice trembled as she tried the endearment out for the first time. "Don't let the tragedy of the past consume you any more. Maybe it would help you to know that mother did try to make amends for what she'd done."

"What do you mean?"

"Because she did something totally out of character for her. She moved us to New York to give me access to the artist's world because she knew I'd inherited a tiny part of your talent. We cleaned office buildings together to earn money."

Her father's stunned expression touched her heart. "Now that you've told me everything, I wonder if she wasn't hoping to bump into you again, which would have been a big step for her. Right before she died, she finally told me your name, that I should always reverence it."

Sam knew he was having difficulty. "Thank you for that, honey," he finally murmured, then looked her straight in the eye. "So now we're back to square one."

For some odd reason, her heart started to act up. "I don't understand."

"Yes, you do. Don't let history repeat itself. Fight for Perseus."

She averted her eyes. "I've already told you the whole story. You can't compare your situation with mother, to mine."

"Something tells me this has very little to do with Sofia, and much more to do with you. Do you really think that phone number was so important, he'd force you into that kind of a bargain if he didn't want something else much more important out of it in return?"

"More important than Sofia?" she gasped.

"Honey—" He was smiling now. "He was in love with my painting. When you appeared in his office, he probably thought he was hallucinating. Do you hear what I'm saying?''

"But he's planning to marry her in a year." She practically moaned the words.

"Is he?"

A tremor passed through her body.

"They haven't been together for twenty years. Love has to be fed. Has Perseus ever come right out and told you he's going to marry her?"

Sam searched her memory, but it was all a confused jumble. "I—I'm sure he has." Her voice throbbed.

"You don't sound very sure to me. Why don't you ask him?"

"I couldn't."

"You mean like your mother couldn't reach out to me when she finally realized she wanted me after all? Don't wait that long for answers, honey. Life's too short."

A terrible fear coupled with a burgeoning excitement took hold of Sam.

Did she dare take her father's advice?

CHAPTER ELEVEN

THE clock said ten after two in the morning. Sam's father had left the villa a little over a half hour ago with the promise that he and Anna would fly to New York within the next couple of weeks so Sam could meet the woman who now held his heart.

Perseus had gone to bed much earlier in the evening, but had been the urbane host at dinner. With his innate sophistication and charm, he'd solicited information from her father about his latest successes and future plans. Sam interjected a comment here and there, but mostly she listened.

It was a great joy to watch the two men she loved most in the world sharing their thoughts about art, about life, sensing their mutual rapport. She soaked it all in, occasionally darting a covert glance at Perseus, the embodiment of a Greek god. Unfortunately the evening ended when her father announced he must be going.

As Sam lay there in the bed wide-awake, she wondered if Perseus was having as much trouble getting to sleep. But more than that, she wondered if she had the temerity to unmask him.

Her mind went over and over the conversation with her father. She didn't think she was like her mother, but maybe she was after all. It took a tremendous amount of confidence to confront the man you loved, and dare to reach out for your happiness.

Perseus and her father had traveled down similar paths, scarred inside and out by the women they'd loved. Yet Anna, who Sam learned was a landscape artist, sounded like she knew exactly what she wanted, and was willing to do anything to be a part of his life for as long as he wanted her in it. *Eleven years...* In the face of such odds, where did she get her courage to fight for a man as complicated as Jules Gregory?

Sam turned on her side, restless, her heart aching. After tonight she knew she couldn't wait eleven days, let alone eleven months for answers. It would be better to know the truth now, and face the hell she was sure of, than wait for the hell yet to come a year from now.

With her heart practically catapulting out of her chest, she swung her feet to the floor and reached for her robe. Moving in bare feet across the tiles to the connecting door, she raised her hand to knock, then couldn't go through with it. If he was asleep, she hated disturbing him.

That's an excuse, Sam.

Taking another fortifying breath, she lifted her hand again and tapped with her knuckles. No sooner had she knocked, than the door opened.

"*Perseus!*" she cried in astonishment because he'd answered so fast. Looking beyond his shoulder she could see that his bed still hadn't been turned down. Maybe he'd been out in the surf and had just come in. He stood inches away from her, wearing his brown robe which he must have hastily thrown on because he was still fastening the belt. She took a step backward.

"I've been expecting you." His somber mood troubled her in ways she couldn't even define.

"Why?" she asked softly, sensing that something was wrong. In the near darkness her eyes searched his, but she couldn't see into them. An uneasy silence prevailed.

"I assumed you might need to talk. It isn't every day that a daughter who has just been united with her long-lost father, must say goodbye to him again so soon."

Perseus always put her needs before his own.

"Y-you're right. It was hard to watch him walk out the door."

But nothing will match the pain when I watch you walk away from me for the last time, my darling.

She felt rather than saw his body stiffen. "I presume he asked you to go back to Sicily with him, and now you want my permission."

Surprised by the unexpected assumption, she was caught off guard. "Actuall—"

"I can't say I blame him." Perseus cut her off abruptly. There was an intensity about him she'd never felt before. "I know that if you were the daughter I'd just found, I would demand that you come home with me."

"I—I think that's your Greek blood talking," she quipped nervously to bring a little levity into the conversation. "My father recognizes I'm not a little girl anymore."

Her attempt at humor didn't phase him or change his forbidding countenance.

"As long as we go together, I don't see that as a problem."

She was incredulous. "But there'd be no reason for you to come."

He stood like an impregnable fortress, his hands in the pockets of his robe. "As far as the world is concerned, we're still on our honeymoon. The press might not be kind to either of us if you left me to go to your father.

"They might see Sofia's departure for Turkey too great a coincidence, and follow me in the hopes of catching us in a compromising position. However, if you and I left on a trip together, no one would think anything about it."

Her heart was racing far too fast. *What did this mean?* Was her father right? Was this idea of traveling together to Sicily prompted by Perseus's need to be with her, because he couldn't bear to let her out of his sight? *If that were true...*

On the other hand, she groaned inwardly, he could still be playing out his part to the bitter end, so there'd be no scandal to hurt his future with Sofia.

She'd knocked on his door to find out those answers. But she didn't know if she had the courage to follow through. If he told her he was more in love with Sofia than ever, and intended on making her his wife, Sam didn't know how she would stand it.

Clearing her throat she said, "I'm afraid this discussion isn't relevant, Perseus. You see, before my father could ask me anything, I begged him to come to New York."

Even the darkness couldn't disguise the jerk of his head, or the frown marring his unforgettable features. She'd said something else wrong because there was another tension-filled pause.

"If you're asking if he can live with us, I see no problem. Not if it is what you want."

"That's incredibly generous of you, Perseus, but I think Anna might have something to say about it. If I'm not mistaken, he's on his way back to Sicily right now to propose marriage to her. I'm hoping that when they come to New York in two weeks for a visit, we'll be able to give them an engagement party."

In the next instant his hands shot out and gripped her upper arms firmly. "Stop it, *Kyria.* Pretend with anyone else, but not with me."

His hands on her body made her lose her concentration. She couldn't think this close to him. "I'm not pretending anything."

He gave her a gentle shake. "Can you honestly stand here and tell me you're not devastated that he has gone away again, when I know what finding him has meant to you?

"Don't forget we were in my room two nights ago when pain stored up over a lifetime came gushing out of you. No one recovers that fast."

"You don't understand, Perseus. Two days ago I was a different person. Two days ago I thought my father knew about me, and had turned his back on me. Today's revelations have changed everything.

"I know he loves me. We're planning on staying close for the rest of our lives. But I'm no longer a child who needs her daddy to tuck her into bed, and read her a story. I have a husband who takes care of me now." She said the last in a trembling voice. It might as well have been a confession of love.

In response, his hands began kneading her shoulders unconsciously. She could feel the tremendous effort he was making to stay in control.

"You've surpassed your performance of the other night. Anyone hearing you would think you were a deliriously happy bride, content to remain with her husband all the rest of her days."

His fingers bit into her arms but she welcomed, craved, the contact. Anything that brought her closer to him.

"You think I don't know the truth?" he bit out in self-deprecation. "You'd sell your soul to be with your father right now."

"You're wrong, Perseus. I'm only staying with you for one reason—" Her voice came out sounding breathless.

"And we both know why. Because that valiant, noble spirit of yours won't allow you to rescind our bargain."

"Not after all the things you've done for me, no. But isn't that what you want? To present the picture of domestic bliss to the world until you can marry Sofia?"

she cried out in fresh pain. Another minute and she'd give herself away completely.

His answer was a long time in coming. "Much as you're hoping for it, *Kyria*, marriage to Sofia isn't going to happen. It was never a possiblity, except in your mind."

Never?

The exquisite joy those words brought was short-lived when his hands suddenly trailed down her arms, then went back to his pockets once more.

She didn't want to hear what was coming next, but a compulsion more powerful than anything she'd ever known in her life wouldn't let her stay silent.

"Why do you say that?" she asked in a barely audible tone. "What has changed? Not your love for her! Surely not her love for you!" It had to be said, and she had to say it, but she couldn't prevent her voice from quivering.

"No, that hasn't changed for either one of us."

Well, Sam. There's your answer. Your father was wrong because he's in love with Anna and wants you to experience that same fulfilling happiness. Don't you dare go to pieces in front of Perseus.

Schooling herself to remain composed, an effort which was costing her dearly, she said in a wooden voice, "Then I don't see the problem."

"That's because I haven't told you everything," he ground out. "She's in agony because she has a son who's in love with a local village girl in Turkey. A rather fitting irony to a bizarre tale, wouldn't you say, *Kyria*?"

While Sam was barely grasping the implications of that revelation Perseus said, "He doesn't want to live in Greece, and Sofia can't bear to live apart from him."

Sam didn't think she could take any more. "I-is he *your* son?" She had to ask the question.

"No," was his emphatic reply.

Another pain he had to endure. He was Greek to his

very soul. It would have meant everything to have a son of his own body. She could scarcely breathe.

"So what you're saying is, that if you two want to be together, you'd have to set up residence in Turkey?"

"Yes," he murmured. "Since that's out of the question for reasons I don't want to go into, it appears I have no more claim on the bargain you and I made in your apartment." A hushed silence prevailed before he said, "You're free to leave and do whatever your heart desires."

Free to leave... The words she'd been dreading.

Her heart almost failed her. If she lived to be a thousand years old, this was one outcome of a situation she could never have imagined being caught up in.

No wonder he'd practically ravished her in the car earlier tonight. He was fighting demons most humans would never have to endure. But he was Perseus, born on the island of Serifos, where the lines of myth and reality were blurred.

On this island, her own father had exorcised her mother from his heart. It was here Perseus had given his heart to Sofia. But his story had rewritten the history books because the only person who'd turned into stone was a grief-stricken Perseus, cursed by the other gods because of his great courage, strength and male beauty.

She had to get out of here.

"Part of our contract is still in effect," came the solemn pronouncement. "I will set you up in business whether it be here, New York or Sicily."

"*Sicily*?" Anger caused her to shout the word at him. "I don't want to live there! To damnation with your contract!"

"But you need someone in your life, Samantha," he spoke on, undaunted. "Your father is prepared to—"

"Enough about my father!" Her entire body was

shaking. "It sounds to me like you can't wait for me to get out of here. If you'll please give me back my passport, and write me a check for ten thousand dollars tonight, I can leave in the morning with no financial worries.

"Keep the prize money when it comes. No one will be able to tell you endorsed my name on the back of the check. Except for the clothes I need to walk out of here, I'll leave everything else. When I get where I'm going, you can send me my fabric swatches and tablecloths.

"Now, if you don't mind—" She stopped to catch her breath. "I'm very tired and would like to go to bed."

"So would I," came the silky voice. "*With my wife.*"

She felt as if a bolt of lightning had just charged her body. Flame licked her cheeks.

"Oh, no. Perseus. You just released me from our contract. I no longer have to be a substitute for Sofia. I was your bride by day, remember?"

"I remember," his voice rasped, "and I've been living in a hell of my own making ever since."

What was he saying now? "Your hell was being torn away from the woman you loved!"

"That's true. Sofia was my first love, the kind of love a boy feels for a lovely, exciting girl when he's on the threshold of becoming a man. But love has to be nurtured, *Kyria.*"

Her father's words.

"Though the feelings I had for her died years ago, naturally she'll always hold a special place in my memory."

"She still loves you."

"The memory of me," he amended. "Like me, she needed to have closure on the past. Now that she's returning to Turkey, she can start a new life. She's a beautiful woman with a great deal of love to give. Some lucky man is going to claim her heart one day, and she has a son she adores.''

''How can you say that so glibly when you've spent your adult life looking for her?'' Her throbbing voice resounded in the bedroom.

''Because I was curious to know why she did what she did, why she disappeared. I halfway suspected it might have been something to do with her father, and worried she could be in serious trouble. When a Greek hates, it is all-consuming, and her father hated me.''

''That's horrible.'' She wanted to reach out and comfort him.

''I agree. I feared he'd take it out on her. As it happens, I wasn't wrong. For a long time I felt guilty for loving her because it brought her to such grief.''

Sam took a step closer and put a tentative hand on his warm, solid arm. ''So *that's* why you were so upset when you couldn't find the phone number.''

''Yes... With all my spy network, I never was able to learn where her father had sent her. When I received word that she was still alive, and possibly trying to make contact with me, the guilt lifted, and all I could feel was profound gratitude.''

Sam's eyes closed tightly. ''To think I shouted at you that my final grade was more important than that phone number...''

Her feelings were in such chaos, it took time to sort everything out until she summoned enough courage to ask the one question haunting her above all else.

''I-if the only emotion you felt was gratitude, then why did you make that contract with me?''

His hands lifted to her hot cheeks, locking her in place. This close, she could see the intensity of his black gaze. ''You want the truth, my sweet, adorable wife?''

''Perseus—please don't be kind to me because you

think you have to. Of course I want the truth! No more lies.''

She felt his muscles tense. "So be it."

The room whirled as he plucked her from the floor and carried her into his bedroom. The dizziness intensified as he lowered her to the mattress, then followed her down with his hard body. Her hands were pinned beneath his above her head.

"You wanted honesty," he whispered between long, drugging kisses that left her witless. "So do I... Tell me if you can why you made a bargain with the devil, one furthermore who was scarred."

"I love your scar," she admitted without thinking, and kissed it. "I felt sorry for you because your love had been so brutally destroyed. I—I suppose I wanted to comfort you."

He lifted his head far enough to look down at her. "I felt sorry for you, too, because I knew some man had hurt you in a way that goes too deep for tears. I found myself wanting to protect you from ever being hurt again. But what you've said doesn't explain why you'd enter into a contract as real and binding as marriage with a stranger."

By now his long, powerful legs had tangled with hers, and he was kissing the creamy smoothness of her shoulder where her robe had slipped down.

"Surely you know I did it because I love you," she murmured against his neck, wanting to communicate words, but needing his touch desperately. "Love was the reason, Perseus. My only reason. You were the man I wanted for my husband. When we said our vows before the priest, I meant them with all my heart. I was willing to do anything to be near you. *Anything!*"

"Then we understand each other perfectly," Perseus whispered against her lips before plundering her mouth once more. "You walked into my office, squeaking with every wet step as you came closer. Like a modern-day Andromeda, wearing jeans and this amazing shirt which had to be an original, it seemed I had literally plucked you from the sea.

"I was in shock because your golden hair and exquisite face were hauntingly familiar. I knew I'd seen you somewhere before. Suddenly I imagined you draped in diaphanous green, and you became the embodiment of the woman in the painting staring down at us.

"Unlike most people who want something from me, you proceeded to vivisect me with that rapier tongue, repudiating me and my possessions with every word coming out of that provocative, delicious mouth I'll crave until death and beyond."

To prove his point, he devoured her thoroughly until she was groaning with need.

"I'm still bleeding from the wounds, *Kyria*, but you're the only elixir provided by the gods to heal them. I was counting on your compassion over my star-crossed love affair, and made up that absurd contract to bind you to me until I could get you to fall in love with me. You know that, don't you?

"You know you're my Andromeda, that I've fallen hopelessly in love with you. *You have to know it*!" he cried in a rush of naked, raw emotion that could leave her in no doubt.

"I've wanted to believe it," she gasped from sheer joy. "My father said that you were in love with me, but—"

"We can thank heaven that Jules is an intelligent man."

"I agree." The words came out muffled because his mouth was driving her over the brink of sanity. "He said that since I was so deeply in love with you, I should ask you if you were truly going to marry Sofia."

"So *that* was the reason for your knock on my door tonight."

"*Yes*, my beloved. I adore you." Her breath caught. "I think I admitted it to myself as early as that scary ride down the elevator of your office building."

A chuckle broke from his throat before he buried his face in her glorious hair.

"It's true. At the time, you reminded me of Hades, whisking me off to your underworld, disobeying all the traffic laws, commandeering my apartment. But I found that I rather liked the way you sort of took over my life. To my shame, when you tempted me with marriage, no matter how bogus, I didn't hesitate to leap right in."

By now his chuckle came rumbling out as full-bodied laughter. The happiest sound in all the world. "*Agape mou*," he murmured in his native tongue. "I knew I loved you when you called me Mr. Kofolopogos. It was then I decided that I was going to have you for myself."

"Thank God," she whispered. Delirious with yearning, she raised her mouth to his, her hunger for him becoming insatiable.

"You wouldn't say that if you knew the sinful thing I was plotting before you came to my room tonight."

She raised her hands to his face and forced him to look at her. "What sinful thing?"

Lines hardened his face in a grimace of self-abnegation. "Normally a stroll along the beach before bed has always been my way of getting in touch with myself, a sort of sanctuary to work things out.

"But tonight there was no solace in the sand or the water. I found myself in the bitterest purgatory because I thought you were going to leave with your father in the morning, and I knew I had no right to prevent you."

A shudder shook his magnificent body. "The worst of it is, I knew I was going to stop you from leaving. I had your kidnapping all planned."

Her eyes widened. "*Kidnapping*?"

He nodded. "In ways I'm even more ruthless and evil than my former stepfather."

"Perseus— Don't say that. You're the most wonderful man I've ever known. It's a privilege to be loved by you, to be your wife."

He shook his dark head. "You haven't heard me out. You may change your mind."

"*Never*! But go on if you have to. Finish telling me your terrible tale," she said with a smile in her voice as she traced the line of his compelling male mouth. She couldn't believe he loved her, that he was hers to love forever.

"There's a tiny, uninhabited island near Tinos. No one goes there. I had this plan to take you back to Athens via the sailboat, which I have well stocked for emergencies.

"En route I had every intention of taking us sailing there. Once we'd pulled up on the beach to eat, I planned to pretend illness so you'd have to nurse me back to health. Your compassionate heart wouldn't have suspected a thing, and I hoped that after a week's time, when I'd fully recovered, you would have admitted your love for me."

His eyes flashed dark fire, giving her a deeper glimpse into the passion igniting his psyche. She experienced a thrill of excitement to think that such a primitive passion burned for her.

"If you hadn't come to your senses by then, I was going to do something really terrible. If necessary, chain you to one of the rocks like Andromeda of old, until you called out your love for me."

Her lips curved bewitchingly. "I know you would never do such a thing. As if you would need to resort to those kinds of measures when I love you so desperately." Her voice caught.

"Samantha—" Once more he captured her mouth, showing her just how much he needed her. They couldn't get enough of each other. "I fear your father's painting has always been my favorite treasure," he eventually murmured against her throat.

"But when you appeared to me in the flesh, it was like Pandora's box had been opened. From that time forth, you became my obsession. Do you think you can handle that? Being the obsession of a man who has laid his heart at your feet? You'll never know how much I wanted to include conjugal rights as part of our marriage contract."

His words created too much happiness. All she could do was embrace him harder. "Why didn't you? I've been aching to make love to you," she confessed openly. "Every time you started making love to me, then stopped, I died a little more inside."

"That's because I prized your love more than anything else in life. If you couldn't give me your beautiful body to worship because you couldn't help yourself, then I wanted no part of forcing you to sleep with me, never knowing if you truly loved me, or were simply sacrificing yourself to fulfill our bargain."

"Oh, Perseus. You'll never know how much I've longed to share your bed. I've yearned for you. Make love to me now, darling. I need you. I love you," she cried from her heart, her voice trembling with desire.

"*Agape mou.*" He crushed her to him, his voice so husky, she didn't recognize it.

"One day, Perseus, I want us to make love on that tiny, uninhabited island."

She heard his groan of satisfaction.

"Honestly, darling—I don't think you could possibly know how jealous I was when you told me about taking Sofia to Delos."

He began kissing every inch of her face and neck.

"Delos is for tourists and lovers, *Kyria*. Everyone goes there. I'd been there with half a dozen girls from the village before I ever met Sofia."

"Perseus!" she cried in mock anger, then threw her arms around his neck, pulling him down so there was no part of them that wasn't touching.

"Well, I want my own island where I can give myself to you wholehearted, over and over again, away from any jealous gods who would try to threaten our happiness."

Feeling suddenly shy, she buried her face in his neck. "I want to give you a son or daughter right away. I want to give you everything. That's the way your love makes me feel."

His chest heaved as he began removing the robe from her body. "If you really want to go, are you prepared to be away several months? That's how long I want you to myself, *Kyria*."

She could feel his impatience to make her his true wife. The fire in his kiss was a promise of the rapture to come. He could have no idea how much she needed to love him, to be loved by him...

"After two months, will you cut my chains, beloved Perseus, and take me to my father to ask for my hand in true marriage?"

Perseus began to smile. It illuminated his face. She wanted to paint him just like this. But not right now. Not when she couldn't think of ever leaving his arms, let alone this bed.

He buried his face in her hair. "You've made me feel immortal. I'm in the mood to grant you your slightest wish."

"Careful, my darling," she whispered. "You know how much trouble you got into the last time you made me that offer."

A low chuckle rumbled out of him, thrilling her. "I

love getting into trouble with you. I want to get into so much trouble, it will take a lifetime and beyond to work everything out.''

''Well… I was thinking we could name our firstborn son, Hercul—''

''*Granted*,'' he murmured against her lips, his kisses becoming more drugging, more primitive. ''Anything else you wish to ask me will have to wait till later. Much, much later.''

Remember the magic of the film
It's a Wonderful Life?
The warmth and tender emotion of
Truly, Madly, Deeply?
The feel-good humor of *Heaven Can Wait?*

Well, even if we can't promise you angels that look like Alan Rickman or Warren Beatty, starting in June in Harlequin Romance®, we can promise a brand-new miniseries: GUARDIAN ANGELS. Featuring all of your favorite ingredients for a perfect novel: great heroes, feisty heroines and a breathtaking romance—all with a celestial spin.

Look for Guardian Angels in:

June 1998: THE BOSS, THE BABY AND THE BRIDE (#3508)
by Day Leclaire

August 1998: HEAVENLY HUSBAND (#3516)
by Carolyn Greene

October 1998: A GROOM FOR GWEN (#3524)
by Jeanne Allan

December 1998: GABRIEL'S MISSION (#3532)
by Margaret Way

Falling in love sometimes needs a little help from above!

Available wherever Harlequin books are sold.

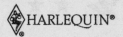

Not The Same Old Story!

HARLEQUIN PRESENTS®

Exciting, glamorous romance stories that take readers around the world.

Harlequin Romance®

Sparkling, fresh and tender love stories that bring you pure romance.

HARLEQUIN Temptation

Bold and adventurous—Temptation is strong women, bad boys, great sex!

HARLEQUIN SUPERROMANCE®

Provocative and realistic stories that celebrate life and love.

Contemporary fairy tales—where anything is possible and where dreams come true.

HARLEQUIN INTRIGUE®

Heart-stopping, suspenseful adventures that combine the best of romance and mystery.

LOVE & LAUGHTER™

Humorous and romantic stories that capture the lighter side of love.